We'll All Be Better People

Short Stories

Paul Bowers

We'll All Be Better People

Acknowledgments

Some of these stories first appeared in the following publications:

"Catbirds." *Windhover: A Journal of Christian Literature*
"Glow." *Southwestern American Literature*
"If Nothing Happens Like It Should." *Indiana Review*
"To Our Own Devices." *Mid-American Review*
"Tortuga Jorge." *Porchlight: A Journal of Southern Literature*

Special thanks to Rilla Askew, for her kind encouragement to "write more fiction," to Ken Hada, for his friendship and poetry, and to Mark Walling, for his invaluable insights.

Book Design: Rowan Kehn

Cover image: Turkey Cock, by Ustad Mansur, opaque watercolor and gold on paper, Mughal, ca. 1612. Public domain.

ISBN: 979-8-9947790-1-9

Turning Plow Press

For Denise,
and for Sydney and Rowan

Contents

Tortuga Jorge 5

So, Do I Hang Up First, or You? 15

Glow 29

I'm in Garrison, Texas 38

Natural Horsemanship 56

To Our Own Devices 65

Catbirds 71

We'll All Be Better People 79

If Nothing Happens Like It Should 89

I think I could turn and live with animals, they
are so placid and self-contain'd,
I stand and look at them long and long.

They do not sweat and whine about their
condition,
They do not lie awake in the dark and weep for
their sins...

~Walt Whitman, *Song of Myself*

Tortuga Jorge

Evaline Bender-Gonzalez was in her backyard burying turtles with a large gravy spoon. She scooped up a helping of black sod and tapped it into a Tupperware bowl like she was serving up an extra thick chocolate pudding. On her knees, crouched on yellow dish towels, she removed a turtle from a box, gingerly planted it in the hole, filled, stood up, moved her towels, scooted the box of turtles with her foot, and stabbed the spoon into the ground again.

Mrs. Koonce watched her from her screened-in patio next door, knowing full well it was her gravy spoon Evaline was ruining for the sake of turtles, and she had spent the last few minutes trying to convince herself that the Tupperware bowl looked awfully familiar as well. But she had too many lids and too many bowls in her life to sort them all out in her head, so she concentrated again on the gravy spoon, which almost certainly belonged to her.

The spoon was part of a set Wiley brought home with him from a business trip to Des Moines—how long ago? Thirty years now?—and there was a porcelain gravy bowl and a butter dish and two spatulas: the pattern—blue flowers, maybe pea vines in a swirl of green. He unpacked so many utensils after his trips she couldn't keep them all straight and the spoons and tongs and long meat forks clanged like wind chimes in her memory. Of course, he didn't actually buy them for her; they were company display samples; she benefited greatly from being the wife of a kitchen utensil salesman, twenty-seven years with the company, and she always had more corn cob holders and colanders and towel hooks than a person would ever need. She had given away or loaned so many Teflon skillets and tenderizing mallets and Miracle egg slicers it would have been impossible to account for them all, but she didn't recall ever loaning Evaline Bender-Gonzalez anything, much less such a large, beautifully curved gravy spoon with a decorative ceramic handle (which she immediately recognized, with her expert eye for utensils, as a rarity), and certainly not for the purpose of burying turtles.

But then Evaline had some strange habits, which Mrs. Koonce knew must have come from her Mexican husband, Jorge, whom Evaline still irritatingly referred to, fifteen years after his death, as her "gravely ill second husband." But Mrs. Koonce much preferred that title to his proper name, which she always saw spelled out in her mind as "W-h-o-r-e-h-a-y."

The cottages were bathed in late autumn sunlight, the breeze off the lake was light and refreshing and smelled faintly of water lilies, and if it had not been for Evaline, still wearing her housecoat and slippers (although it was well past ten o'clock) stooping over her little holes and scattering turtles like so many rough stones around her yard, it might have been a nice day. When it came right down to it, Mrs. Koonce thought, she was there first, a full three years before Evaline, and if her sister Lucille hadn't died unexpectedly in the airplane lavatory on her way to Georgia, Mrs. Koonce would have had the neighbor she wanted, and deserved. In fact, until Evaline Bender-Gonzalez moved into the retirement community just outside Athens, Mrs. Koonce was having what she considered a run of very good luck. She outmaneuvered a couple from Canada for the cottage with a better view of the lake, Lucille's husband, Manny, died in his sleep, and the cottage next door was miraculously hammered and wired and painted into completion while Mrs. Koonce was away comforting Lucille in Flagstaff. It was as if Wiley was in heaven looking out for her, working deals, expediting paperwork, selling God on the idea that it would better for everyone if Manny were called home sooner rather than later. And he must have gotten to Lucille as well, for although she stubbornly swore she would never leave Flagstaff, two weeks after Manny's funeral she transferred her savings to a credit union in Athens and hired a moving van.

Now, with Lucille's entire household moldering in storage somewhere in Dallas where her daughter lived, all of Mrs. Koonce's dreams of summer walks with her sister by the lake and shared potluck dinners at the clubhouse dwindled away, and she was saddled with Evaline, who mostly kept to herself and watched ice-skating on TV and buried hapless amphibians in her backyard with heisted gravy spoons. And Wiley, who was so helpful before, had apparently lost interest in the affairs of her earthly life and left her to chance. Or maybe he simply lost his touch and couldn't close a deal.

No, Mrs. Koonce thought, smoothing her green blouse of wrinkles the community laundress spitefully added with the iron, life was not turning out well at all.

She stirred her chamomile tea and leaned forward in her cane and wicker chair. Evaline lifted another turtle from the cardboard box and held it away from her body to avoid a sudden stream of pee.

Mrs. Koonce knew a person couldn't just saunter up and ask another to please stop burying turtles in her own backyard, and she certainly would not offer to help merely as a ploy to gain an explanation. The gravy spoon, she decided, was her best bet. She could talk kitchen utensils with anyone, even with the detached Evaline Bender-Gonzales, with whom she had absolutely nothing in common except geographical location, which never would have happened to begin with if her sister Lucille had taken the bus.

She changed into her lavender jogging suit and pearl white leather sneakers to make it look like she was simply out for a walk. She went out the front door and followed the sidewalk that bent between the cottages, swinging her arms high to mimic serious cardiovascular exercise and then quick-stepped alongside the fence. She found Evaline standing with a turtle in one hand and the gravy spoon in the other, looking puzzled.

Mrs. Koonce strode into Evaline's line of sight, then wheeled suddenly, putting on her best look of surprise and sheer neighborly delight. "Good morning, Eva," she said, breaking her greeting with breathlessness for effect.

"Adele," Evaline said absently, as if she had just been startled out of a nap.

"Out for a little jaunt," Mrs. Koonce said. "Would you like to take a lap around the lake? I could use the company."

"This yard is very, very small," Evaline said.

Now that Mrs. Koonce was nearby, she saw the dark little graves scattered about the yard. "Sweetheart, you have moles," she said, tried a deep-knee bend but managed only a shallow squat that made her ankles hurt.

"I had a much bigger place in Sarasota. Jorge, my gravely ill second husband, bought two lots there."

Mrs. Koonce bent at the waist, aimed her fingers toward her toes, which seemed much further away than they used to be, and hid her grimace. For Evaline to use both her husband's designations in one sentence was almost more than she could bear, but when she straightened up, all indications of disgust were wiped clean. "Wherever did you find that lovely spoon? I've seen only one like it in all my years," Mrs. Koonce said.

Evaline shifted her attention to the gravy spoon, clotted with dirt. Her fingers were dark and muddy, her housecoat stained at the knees, house shoes half off her feet. The turtle shell she held slowly sprouted legs and a head and Evaline clacked its round back with the spoon to force it to withdraw. "No, no," she said.

Mrs. Koonce, no longer able to feign ignorance, said, "Why, Evaline, you have a turtle in your hand," then extended her arms at shoulder height and made small circles in the air.

Evaline watched her, and Mrs. Koonce again bent at the waist, left and right. Her fake exercises were beginning to feel genuine.

"I've got more," Evaline said, using the gravy spoon to point at the scattering of little mounds. "It's time for them to hibernate, but I'm afraid I'm running out of space. They mustn't be crowded together. Too easy for foxes to find them."

Mrs. Koonce had never seen a fox anywhere in the vicinity, and she couldn't imagine how a fox would go about eating a turtle even if one should miraculously find its way into Evaline's backyard.

"I don't suppose," Evaline said, "we could put these last two in your yard?"

Mrs. Koonce lifted one knee as high as she could, then the other. This wasn't what she expected, but then she was having a streak of bad luck equal to, if not worse than, her earlier pattern of good fortune that handed her the cottage with a view and a sister on her way from Arizona.

Mrs. Koonce brought her aerobics to a sudden halt, pushed her hair off her forehead. She was, at the very least, disappointed in her husband. He left her stranded for more than five years, and now he burdened her with the task of recovering her gravy spoon and keeping turtles out of her backyard. "I'm sure if you put them down they'll find a place on their own," she said flatly. "You can let them go by the lake where the ground is softer. And wouldn't that be a nice place for them to wake up?"

But Evaline brought up the foxes, and the hordes of grandchildren who arrived on weekends and holidays and tore through the community looking for something to get into, and, she said, they were sure to dig them up and use them to play catch, or even throw them in the lake.

Mrs. Koonce found herself completely out of exercises and still without the spoon, and since she could think of no reasonable objection to dropping the two remaining turtles in a far corner of her lawn, she offered to carry Evaline's towel and bowl, and of course the spoon, while Evaline carried the turtles.

Once she had the spoon in her hand, she knew that it was not at all like the one Wiley gave her. It was lightweight, the handle plastic instead of ceramic, the pattern blue cornflower, not pea vine—clearly, five-and-dime material. Worst of all, she suddenly remembered that she gave the entire set—bowl, butter dish, spoon—to Lucille, and it was most likely boxed up in some corner of the dusty storage facility in Dallas. But Evaline was already through the gate and Mrs. Koonce couldn't very well call her back.

"Do you think they'll mind being separated from . . . the herd?" Mrs. Koonce asked, unable to think of the proper term for a group of turtles.

"Oh, they aren't gregarious," Evaline said. "They go to sleep alone and wake up alone." She put the box down near the rose bush, and scuffed at the grass with her bare heel.

"If that's the standard," Mrs. Koonce said, handing her the gravy spoon, "I'm not gregarious either."

Evaline dug, expertly, efficiently, and had both turtles in the ground and covered up in a matter of minutes. She stood up, wiped her hands with the towel, worked her feet fully into her slippers and dropped the spoon, handle-first, into the pocket of her housecoat.

Mrs. Koonce stared at the small disturbances in her otherwise pristine lawn. "What if they crawl back out?" she asked. "What if they don't want to be buried just yet?"

"They must be buried," Evaline said emphatically. "It's time," then, "Would you like me to join you for coffee?"

Mrs. Koonce thought, no, I wouldn't, now that the gravy spoon issue had been resolved, but she had always been the hospitable sort, and although Evaline was hardly dressed properly for socializing, she would not allow herself to be rude.

She opened the patio screen door and directed Evaline to the big wicker chair while she went inside and made coffee and arranged sugar cookies on a plate. She took cups and saucers, her everyday ware, from the cabinet above. She was out of cream but found a couple of sugar packets and placed them on the saucers, along with teaspoons.

She returned to the patio to find Evaline had removed her house shoes and was staring intently at her toes, which she wriggled against the linoleum.

"Here we are," Mrs. Koonce said quickly, hoping to distract Evaline so that she wouldn't actually start cleaning her feet and then dig around the cookie plate. "I hope you don't mind drip."

Evaline said, "Jorge liked instant and I like drip. I despise instant."

"This isn't instant," Mrs. Koonce said, "it's drip."

"Drip is best," Evaline said.

"Have a cookie or two as well."

Evaline took a cookie and dunked it in the cup of coffee and tongued the soggy portion into her mouth.

"I'm sorry I'm out of cream," Mrs. Koonce said.

"Do you have milk?"

"Would you like some milk?"

"No," Evaline said. "Not really."

"I have milk if you want it."

"Just sugar is fine."

"Are you sure?" Mrs. Koonce asked, exasperated over the lack of cream and not knowing if she had any milk anyway.

"Perfectly sure," Evaline said.

"Coffee is something that is often over prepared, if you asked me," Mrs. Koonce said.

"I know what you mean" Evaline said. "Also, if you have to put ketchup on something to eat it, then chances are you don't really like what you're about to eat. Of course, I cannot eat turtle soup anymore either, with or without ketchup."

To which Mrs. Koonce muttered, "Who can?" then, "I can't say I've ever had it, and don't think I'd like it if I did."

"The flavor is wonderful," Evaline said. "It's very sweet, which is always a surprise to anyone who tries it for the first time. My first husband always had a bowl when he traveled to the French Quarter. My second husband, Jorge, who was so gravely ill for so long, wouldn't touch it because of Tortuga Hombre."

"Was he a friend of your gravely . . . of your husband," Mrs. Koonce stumbled, "this Tortilla?"

Evaline laughed. "Tortuga. You say it like this: *Tore-Two-Gah*, but roll the 'r' in *tore*, like in *toro*." She made the sound of a drum roll with her tongue, and a fragment of unswallowed cookie dislodged from somewhere in her mouth and flew to the collar of her robe. "And Tortuga Hombre is not really a person, just a character in an old, old story. Well, I suppose he is like a person, but only like Bugs Bunny is a person."

"Bugs Bunny is a rabbit," Mrs. Koonce said.

"And Tortuga Hombre is a turtle, but also a man," and then Evaline demonstrated how one should also roll the "r" in *hombre*. "Say it with me," she said.

Mrs. Koonce was decidedly against rolling any letters of the alphabet, preferring instead to pronounce them properly; and saying the letters otherwise, she thought, only leads to cookie particles landing on collars. "I'm afraid I have no talent for foreign languages, Eva. And," she added, "Bugs Bunny is a rabbit who only happens to talk."

"Six in one hand," Evaline said. "I don't know much about rabbits, though. I *am* sure that Tortuga Hombre is a man and a turtle, however. That's why I have to bury them."

"Bury who?"

"The turtles. It is because of Tortuga Hombre that they must be buried. Well, not exactly because of it—rather, because Jorge"—and here she deliberately rolled the 'r' in his name—"told me the story once to explain why he would not eat turtle soup. After he passed, I couldn't help but think that the risk of eating one's husband in the process is far too great, so therefore I no longer eat turtle soup either."

"With or without ketchup," Mrs. Koonce added, thinking she might be catching up to Evaline's meandering logic, hoping for a thread to guide her, but she wasn't sure where husbands fit in, or even if she heard correctly. Rather than pursue the matter any further, she offered Evaline another cookie and took another for herself.

"You don't know the story," Evaline said matter-of-factly, and put the cookie back on the plate (which, Mrs. Koonce noted to herself, would be tossed in the trash once Evaline had gone home). "Your husband was not from Mexico, was he?"

Mrs. Koonce almost said *Certainly not*, but bit the cookie and her response in one snip of her teeth and merely shook her head.

"Let me tell it," Evaline said, leaning back into the chair. "There was a poor woman whose husband was too ill to fish, and since her children were hungry and there was nothing in the house except for a handful of corn, she had to do something. So she took her husband's net and the corn and set out one morning just as the sun was coming over the mountains and made her way to the lake.

"At the water's edge, she tossed a few of the precious corn kernels into the shallows and watched the water's surface for ripples, which would indicate the fish were eating the corn, and then she could throw the net and draw them in. But before she made a cast, she heard someone say, 'Please, may I have a kernel of corn, for I and my children are starving.'

"She could see no one, only a turtle resting on a log nearby, so once again she swung the net behind her, but before she could fling it outward, the voice said again, 'Please, may I have a kernel of corn, for I and my children are starving.' This time, she turned quickly enough to see the turtle's sharp beak moving and realized it was the animal that had spoken."

"Tell me, Eva," Mrs. Koonce interrupted, "what does one call a group of turtles?"

"*That*," said Evaline, who had closed her eyes and apparently had no intention of opening them, "is a completely different matter. More importantly, the poor woman told the turtle that she had only enough corn to draw the fish and no more. So the turtle slid off the log into the water and disappeared without another word.

"After many hours, the poor woman had managed to catch only

three very small fish, but it would have to do, so she gathered up the net and made her way back home, where she made a weak fish soup for her family and her gravely ill husband.

"The following day her husband was even worse, so the poor woman took the net and a few kernels of corn and walked to the lake. And what do you think she found but the turtle that had spoken to her the previous day, sitting on the same log."

Mrs. Koonce stared at her empty coffee cup. "How many days does this story last?"

"Three days total," Evaline said, and Mrs. Koonce hoped she didn't mean three days to tell it. "But the third day is just like the first and second. Only this time, the turtle re-appears in the water a few feet from the shore and tells the poor woman that when she arrives home, she will find that her gravely-ill husband has died in bed and that she is left alone in the world to take care of her children. But," Evaline said dramatically, "the turtle tells her that her husband will be reborn as a turtle, and that she must always be respectful to all of their kind because she will not know which one her husband is."

When Evaline finished, she reached for the last cookie, saving Mrs. Koonce the trouble of throwing it away, and put on her house slippers. Mrs. Koonce held her cup of coffee to her lips, although it was empty, not sure what to make of it all, but before she could take a pretend sip, Evaline's expression suddenly changed. Her face puckered, her cheeks blushed, she took a long, staggered breath, and began to cry.

"Eva?" Mrs. Koonce asked, but the name came out in a whisper and Evaline didn't even look at her. Instead, she stared at the cookie in her hand, then placed it gently back on the plate. "Would you like some water?"

Evaline shook her head, and pulled the collar of her robe tight against her throat.

Mrs. Koonce started to offer her a tissue but realized she only had toilet paper, which didn't seem right to offer, or a dish towel, which she didn't want to offer.

Evaline said, "I think I'll just go home," then nodded as if agreeing with her own decision to leave.

"Do you want me to walk over with you? Just to your door, I mean?"

"I'll be fine," she said, finally looking Mrs. Koonce in the eye. It was a strange look. Not Evaline's usual look, which Mrs. Koonce often thought of as removed. "I'm just a little tired from burying things, I guess."

"I would imagine so," Mrs. Koonce agreed, but another thought occurred to her that made her own face feel suddenly warm, but before she could clear her head enough to know what it was, or to say anything else, Evaline shuffled out the screen door without so much as a wave, without so much as a good-bye.

Mrs. Koonce couldn't sleep that night and the darkness wore on slowly. She tried pacing in the living room to tire herself out. She read passages from the Bible, Old Testament genealogies, but even that didn't work.

After another hour of tossing on her mattress and twisting the sheets into knots she went out on her patio and rocked. The night was still and quiet, the moon absent. Mrs. Koonce suddenly felt very lonely. Lucille's daughter had promised to visit at Christmas but nothing more had come of it, and the last connection she had to family was a thinning thread that was sure to break soon, if it hadn't already.

Worst of all, she was suddenly having trouble breathing. She put on her housecoat and house slippers and walked in a panic next door. She knocked quietly, then, after a few minutes, loudly, but Evaline didn't wake up. No light came on in the house.

Mrs. Koonce was sure an artery was about to break in her head. Her face grew warm again. The utensils in her mind rang violently as if caught in a hurricane. She made it back to her patio, only to discover the back door that led into the kitchen was locked. She felt in her housecoat pockets but realized that her key was hanging on the hook by the sink. She walked around and tried the front door, but it was locked as well.

Mrs. Koonce settled into her rocking chair on the patio. She had no way of knowing the time, only that it was late, and morning still hours away. She knew she'd have to walk to the community office in her housecoat and slippers and ask for the emergency key. It would be fully light by then and her neighbors would see her. There was nothing she could do to make it look like she was just out for an early stroll around the lake, shuffling along the path, half dressed, hair uncombed.

Somehow, she thought, this was Evaline's fault for digging holes with a gravy spoon. It was the fault of the turtles who cannot apparently survive winter above ground, even in Georgia. It was Lucille's fault for dying at 30,000 feet. It was Wiley's fault for leaving her alone for so long. It was the fault of the woman who would not spare a few kernels of corn.

She recalled the expression on Evaline's face and realized it was the same look she saw on her sister Lucille's face after Manny died. She imagined it must have been an expression she, too, had worn over the years, after Wiley, without even knowing it was there.

She finally fell into an uncomfortable sleep, occasionally opening her eyes just long enough to see it wasn't yet morning.

It was the cracking sound that startled her awake just before dawn. At first she thought it was the rocking chair, its wooden joints popping in the cool of the night. Or maybe someone trying to open the patio door. Maybe even Evaline come at last to help her.

But then she saw the fox—no bigger than a large cat, red as a flame, and in its grinning narrow mouth, caged in teeth, a turtle. Motionless, it stared at her through the thin screen door.

She felt herself rock forward to get out of the chair, but the fox was already gone. She thought she might at least be able to make out the fox going over her fence, but she saw nothing and heard nothing. There was only the night hanging over her house and the silent lake beyond.

Mrs. Koonce got out of her chair, felt herself walk unsteadily through the thinning darkness to her rose bush in the backyard. She went slowly to her knees. She felt the ground for the two tiny mounds where Evaline buried the turtles. When she touched the loose earth of one mound she was sure something moved beneath her fingers. She leaned over and whispered, "Wiley? Is that you?" and felt the earth for a reply.

So, Do I Hang Up First, or You?

The special relationship between the domesticated dog and human beings is at least 15,000 years in duration. Fortunately, *Canis lupus* and *Homo sapiens* never reached the point at which the two species sought a divorce, and at times over our long history together, it seems we are more capable of maintaining our alliance with the genus *Canis* than we are with members of our own species.
Dr. Philip Pettigrew, *A History of Canine Evolution*

Karns watches Mitzi sleep. She is on her back in the corner of the room, her broken front leg, in a cast and bandaged in blue wrap, is upraised, stiff, like she is waiting to be called upon. She snuffles occasionally, writhes, but does not open her eyes.

The vet said she should fully recover in a few months. There were no internal injuries. Yet, despite the vet's positive outlook, Karns half expects her to die in the night, and he makes no deliberate effort to stay awake to witness it. In the morning, he thinks, he'll wrap her in a plastic garbage sack, put her out on the curb, and that will be that.

Still, he keeps the light on, dozes in the recliner, wakes up sporadically without knowing how long he's slept, and each time sees that she is breathing.

He was speeding, and slightly high. Somewhere in that there arises a moral obligation that lingers even after the buzz has worn off and you realize there were no witnesses and no visible damage to the car that neighbors might ask about. Naming the dog after his ex-wife is a cruel whim, but one he decides not to reverse even after he has sobered. It makes him feel better, although it does nothing for the dog, and Mitzi, the human Mitzi, knows nothing of it, and will not suffer in the least.

By the time the front window of his apartment reddens with dawn it is clear that Mitzi isn't going to die after all, that he won't need to put her on the curb, that he'll have to go to the grocery store for food for both of them, that he'll have to shell out additional money on his security deposit to cover any peeing or vomiting.

Oliver Karns makes coffee for himself, then fills a bowl with water for the dog. Her tail wags when he comes near, but she doesn't drink.

His divorce was uneventful. With a signature came the sudden subtraction of a spouse, the addition of a moderately priced furnished apartment with neutral carpet, neutral couch, refrigerator, dishwasher, lamps, pizza three times a week (five counting leftovers for breakfast, usually pepperoni on thin crust), a late-model Buick Century, and a surprising amount of time on his hands that he had yet to fully account for or make use of.

With the dog, however, came an odd return to familiarity—like her human namesake, she took up more than her fair share of the bed, demanded attention during odd hours of the night or when he was feverishly grading exams, wanted to go out early Saturday mornings when he could finally sleep in, showed signs of a distaste for his cooking, demonstrated little interest in his choice of television programs, sat or slept in his favorite chair, occasionally came too close, crowded him, or stared coldly at him from across the room.

She is a mix, a mutt. Mitzi, the ex, is herself German, English, and claims a touch of Jamaican, though she has no outward features to suggest the latter is true—only illicit family rumors involving a distant slave trader and drunken attacks below decks. He knows little about dog breeds, but guesses that she—Mitzi, the canine—is Corgi plus something, plus something else. She has short legs, a large triangular head, upright ears, but lacks the barrel body and coloration of Corgis he's seen. She is midnight black but for an irregular patch of silver on her chest. She is healthy, aside from the leg fracture, which means she was perfectly healthy before her encounter with Karns.

Mitzi, the ex, claims that she, too, was once the picture of health, of mid-western girlhood though already in her late twenties when they married, but that Karns ruined her by not being thoroughly engaging when she needed it the most. "You were once a very interesting person," she had said, then added, "relatively speaking."

Relative to what, he didn't ask. To his former self, perhaps? Or relative to her father (a physician who served time for insurance fraud), or the uncle of an uncle of a great-grandmother who once cruised the coast of Africa for human prey?

Mitzi licks his hand when he sleeps. Mitzi waits for him at the door and follows him, limping, obedient, committed, to the kitchen, the bathroom. She wags her tail a thousand times a day.

Mitzi, the ex, is far away in another state, and, he suspects, rarely thinks of him.

Two weeks after he moved into the apartment, and a few months before the dog arrived, his ex-wife showed up at his door unannounced with an unglazed Bundt cake still in its fluted pan. She said she ran out of confectioners' sugar. She had a plastic grocery bag hanging from her wrist like a purse.

"So, you came to borrow a cup of sugar?"

"That's what's in the bag. I went by the store on the way here," she said, placing the cake on his small kitchen table. "I need a big platter to flip it over on, though, then I'll make the glaze."

"I don't have a platter," he said.

"How can you not have a platter?" She went to the kitchen cabinets and opened each one, leaving the doors ajar as she went down the line. Four bowls, two drinking glasses, two plates and two saucers, two coffee mugs, a bag of ground coffee and filters. Most of the cabinets had no content at all.

Karns opened the doors below the sink and took out the one sauce pan he owned, a sheet pan, and a small cast iron skillet. "We have this to work with," he said.

"The sheet pan and a bowl will do," she said.

He handed her the sheet pan and took a soup bowl from the cabinet.

Mitzi removed the bag of sugar and a bottle of vanilla extract from the grocery bag, along with the sifter, some butter, and a pint of whole milk. She sifted the sugar into the bowl, added milk, hot water, then stirred with a tablespoon (although she said she really needed a whisk, which he also didn't have), until the mixture thickened.

"Looks like glue," Karns said.

Mitzi kept stirring. "Don't you remember when we made a holiday gingerbread house? We took it to your mother's Christmas party?"

"I don't."

Mitzi stopped stirring, put the tip of her finger in the mix and tasted it. "Well, it was this that held the house together. Roof and walls."

"I don't remember that."

"I'm not surprised," she said. "She hated me, and you tend to block out anything unpleasant. It's your special power." Mitzi flipped the cake onto the sheet pan, spooned the glaze over the cake in slow drizzles.

"I have no special powers. Just a certain amount of blissful ignorance."

"You do have that," Mitzi said. She held the spoon with sugar glaze out to him. He took it.

"Sugary."

"Plates and forks, please" she said. "And coffee wouldn't hurt either."

They ate cake and sipped coffee without speaking. When she took
her last bite of her slice, Karns gathered up plates and forks and placed
them in the dishwasher. He topped off their coffee, then sat back
down.

"So, what brings you here? Other than an excuse to eat cake."
She picked up the coffee cup with both hands and took two sips. He
remembered telling her once that she held a coffee cup like a
frostbitten climber rescued from a ledge, the hot liquid the very breath
of life itself.

"Can't a person visit another person just to share some dessert and
chat?"

Karns said, "I thought divorce was precisely what called for the
end of such moments."

"But we never ate Bundt cake together. Not in all our years. Can
you imagine? Old territory is a hard road to travel, but this is entirely
new territory we're in. That's the difference."

Karns stood up and poured the remaining coffee in his cup into
the sink, then put the cup back in the cabinet.

"You aren't going to toss that in the dishwasher?" Mitzi asked.

"I'm the only one drinking out of it, so what's the diff?"

Mitzi got up, rinsed her cup, and put it in the dishwasher.

She sat back down at the table. Karns said, "We all have our little
strategic moves to make, right Mitz?" She didn't answer. "Speaking of
kitchen ware," Karns finally said, "I'm a little shy on some items. If I
recall, we had two can openers, an electric and a manual. You think I
can have one of them? I'll take the manual one. And I could use a
spatula and a soup ladle. Maybe a couple of oven mitts. I can swing by
tomorrow if that's OK with you?"

Mitzi said, "Of course you would be welcome to them. But I'm
afraid everything is, at this very moment, in a moving van heading to
Taos."

Karns thought for a second, said flatly, "That's an odd place to
keep them."

"I just thought I should tell you in person," she said. "Angel has
asked me to move in with her."

Angel, Mitzi's older sister, was one of the few members of Mitzi's
family he actually liked. She was, like him, a high school teacher. In her
case, recently retired. And although she taught English and he taught
science, they always had that shared battleground of teaching in the
public school system. They even talked on the phone quite often. They
talked the week the divorce papers were signed, and Angel invited him
to come visit her in the mountains. The fact that Mitzi was moving to

Taos to live with her explained why Angel hadn't called in a while. "You don't do well at altitude," Karns said. "Remember you got sick when we tried to drive Pikes Peak? We had to turn around on that narrow road and head closer to sea level."

"I'll adjust," Mitzi said. "I've gotten quite good at adjusting."

"And the house?" Karns asked.

"That's another thing. I think we should rent it out. We just turn the key over to a rental agency, and they take care of everything. We get a steady cash flow without much effort. Unless of course you want to live there? I figured it was too much house for you to manage alone. You have a nice place here. With a little sprucing up, it will be cozy."

"Sure it will," Karns said. "With kitchen utensils."

Mitzi reached across the table and took his hand. He felt like pulling away, but he didn't. Her hands were soft. He had always loved the softness of her hands.

"You can keep the Bundt pan, and the sifter," she said. "It'll make for a good start."

Karns has seven sick days left, so he turns in his request to Principal Stewart the Monday after the dog arrives.

"All seven?" Principal Stewart asks. "In a row?" He has his reading glasses wedged on his forehead. In fact, Karns can't remember ever seeing the glasses resting on the bridge of his nose.

"Yes," Karns answers.

"So, you anticipate being sick for the next seven days? But starting tomorrow?"

"Not exactly," Karns says. "It's more of caretaker situation. But I'm out of personal days."

"Someone else is sick?"

Karns says, "There was an accident."

Principal Stewart removes his reading glasses from his forehead and chews on the earpiece. "Family?"

"It's Mitzi," Karns says, lowering his gaze. "She's suffered a significant leg injury."

Principal Stewart drops his glasses on the desk. "I'm sorry to hear that, Oliver. What happened, if you don't mind my asking?"

Karns leans back in the chair and lets out a sigh. "She was in town to visit an old friend and to meet our rental agent. She was just out for a walk in the old neighborhood and some guy sideswiped her. Knocked her into the ditch. Broken tibia."

"Oh my," Principal Stewart says. He is holding the sick leave form in his hand, moving it closer, then farther from his face to find the right distance to read the small print. "I'll ask Miss Tatum to send flowers on behalf of the teachers and staff. Which hospital is she in?"

Karns hesitates, then says, "She's currently staying in my apartment. She's in a cast."

Principal Stewart puts his reading glasses on his forehead, then, to Karns's surprise, drops them to the bridge of his nose, tilts his head back to peer through the thick half lenses. "That must be a little awkward, given your recent separation?"

"At times," Karns says. "But frankly, Mr. Stewart, we are all we've got. Me and Mitzi. Just each other, you know?"

Principal Stewart nods, removes his reading glasses, takes a pen from a coffee cup full of pens, and signs the form.

The next day at the pet store, he puts Mitzi in a shopping cart. He buys canned and dry dog food. He buys treats that look like real bacon. He buys a brush and comb set, a collar and matching leash. He buys a three-pack of tennis balls, though he doesn't know if she knows how to play fetch. He buys a purple hippopotamus stuffed toy because she seems interested in it when he holds it out to her.

At home, he rolls a tennis ball across the kitchen floor. She sniffs at it as it passes by and watches it until it stops under the kitchen table. He rolls another by her, and she ignores it completely.

He puts her on the couch and places the purple hippo between her paws, then waits. She rolls over and goes to sleep.

He gathers his laundry and walks to the complex laundromat. He has the place to himself during the wash until a young woman comes in when he is loading the dryer. She has a black garbage bag in her hand and unloads clothes from a dryer three down from his into the bag, then leaves. He watches his clothes tumble. He eats a bag of barbeque potato chips from the vending machine.

When he returns to his apartment, Mitzi meets him at the door, the purple hippo in her mouth. He pats her head.

The following week, his sick leave days exhausted, he walks into his classroom. On his desk he finds a stack of get-well cards from colleagues, all addressed to Mitzi, including a giant card signed by all twenty-three sixth-period students. He finds handwritten notes from the substitute, saying that classes have gone well all week except when

Dylan Pyles threw a partially dissected frog against the wall just to see if it would stick. And there are quizzes over cell structure, cell division, and cell transport. He grades half during his planning period and puts the rest in his desk drawer.

During cafeteria duty he sits at a table with Peter Hawkins, a history teacher and softball coach, eats an egg salad sandwich he brought from home, while Peter complains about the summer sports camps he got roped in to. "As if I didn't spend enough time with these fuckers during the year," he says. "I had summer plans. Those went to full-on-no-go in a hurry."

Karns asks him what his plans were. Peter says, "Plans not to be here," then, "So, how's the ex-Mrs. Karns? She healing up?"

"Yes," Karns says. "Nicely, I think."

Peter takes a swig of chocolate milk from a carton he lifted when the cafeteria manager had her back turned. "Do you sleep on the couch, or what? Or maybe you have a trundle for yourself?"

"Just the one bed."

Peter leans over. "Really? Even with the divorce and all. Bound to be just a little spark left over, I suppose."

Karns shakes his head. "No. Nothing like that."

"Sure, sure," Peter says. He stirs a plastic spoon around in a small cup of apple sauce. "I get it. Just a matter of convenience, right?" He eats the last spoonful of apple sauce, then says, "My ex would use a leg cast to kick the shit out of me while I slept."

At the end of the day, Karns gathers up the ungraded exams, a few notes to work on his lesson plans, and drives home. When he opens his apartment door it is the odor he notices first, then the foam stuffings scattered across the living room floor and into the kitchen, then the two partially destroyed couch cushions, then the scattered black spots of runny dog shit on the carpet. Mitzi is sitting in the hallway, head lowered, half her leg cast shredded to the mid-joint.

Dr. Wallace has Mitzi on the exam table, stethoscope against her belly. Karns sits in a chair in the corner and watches. He worries she has eaten couch stuffing, or maybe found a joint he lost behind the bed. He is still trying to decide if he bought and smoked all five or only four of the pre-rolls he purchased at the World of Weed drive-thru. The vet takes the earpieces out and hangs the stethoscope around his neck. "Good gut sounds," he says. "How's her appetite?"

"She eats all I give her."

"Any change in food brand?"

Karns shakes his head.

"Do you give her table scraps?"

"Pizza crust. Sometimes at breakfast."

The doctor starts feeling along the tattered cast. "What kind?"

"Usually pepperoni, but we'll go for regular cheese on BOGO days."

"Any with onions?"

"No," Karns says. "My stomach is acidic."

"Bad for dogs, too," he says. "Everybody knows not to give dogs chocolate, but onions? Makes them anemic. I had a client in here the day after New Years with a hungover German Shepherd. Lapped up four vodka martinis left on a serving cart. She found him passed out in her bed along with her mother-in-law."

Karns is on the verge of asking about the effects of cannabis if consumed by a dog, but the vet says Mitzi seems fine, and is likely just nervous being left alone all day. "We'll need to re-do the cast," he says. Then he asks Karns to take a seat in the waiting room. They'd bring Mitzi out to him when they were done.

He sits a few chairs down from a man in dress uniform. What branch of service, he doesn't know, but he sits straight and holds a leash attached to the smallest dog Karns has ever seen. The dog sits perfectly still between the man's immaculately polished shoes. The dog looks like a stuffed toy.

"Mind me asking about your dog?"

The man turns to Karns. "Teacup Shih Tzu."

"What's its name?"

The man tugs slightly on the leash. "Killer," he says.

Karns rubs his face to hide his smile. "That fits," he says.

The man leans over, scoops up the dog, which is barely larger than his palm, and puts it in his lap. "Not really," he says. "My wife named her Sugar Baby." He gently pats the dog's tiny head. "But when we travel together, she's Killer."

"Understandable," Karns says, then, "Navy?"

The man puts the dog back down on the floor. "Southwest."

"Sorry," Karns says. "I'm not good at uniforms."

"No worries. Happens all the time. When I'm not in the airport, people stop me and say, 'Thank you for your service.' Want to shake my hand. It's fucking humiliating, really. And the sad thing is, I don't correct them anymore. I just say, 'You're welcome.' Makes them feel good about themselves."

A woman in red scrubs comes out of an exam room with a clipboard. "Miss Sugar Baby?" The man leans over for the dog, cradles her against his chest. He stands up, nods to Karns, and follows the woman into the room.

It is already 6:30 PM. The waiting room is empty of patients. The receptionist behind the tall counter is shuffling papers into file folders and sliding them into a long wall of hundreds of multi-colored file folders. She occasionally looks at Karns and smiles a tired smile.

Fifteen minutes later, the pilot and Miss Sugar Baby come out of the exam room. The dog has a tiny pink bow on her head now. He pays the bill. On his way out he says to Karns, "Last man standing, eh?"

"Yes," Karns says.

"Hold the line," the pilot says, and pushes the clinic door open.

Karns gets up to ease the stiffness in his back. Beyond the waiting area are shelves of pet food in bags and cans: dog food for large or small breeds, for healthy digestion, weight management, skin and coat, high protein for active dogs, low carb for mature, less active dogs. There is an equal variety of options for cats. They also offer food for fish, gerbils, parakeets, and goats. On a corner shelf, there are dog and cat toys, and a coat tree hung with a dozen leashes with matching collars.

Along the wall opposite is a large bulletin board filled with photos of dogs and cats, pictures drawn by children in crayon and marker of dogs and cats, along with notes of thanks highlighted with hearts and balloons.

Thank you for taking care of Buddy.

Dr. Wallace is the best! Libby the cat loves you! And so do we!

In our moment of loss, you comforted us. Thank you, Doc Wallace.

Best vet ever! Hugs and kisses!

There are flyers for pet grooming services, pet sitters, affordable pet insurance, dog walkers, horse trainers, coupons for nutritional supplements.

Karns sees, in the top corner of the board, tacked on top of a *Free Puppies* flyer with tearaway tabs with a phone number, a photo of a dog he immediately recognizes as Mitzi. He scans the words: *Lost... Answers to Maggie... In vicinity of... Reward... The Davis Family... misses very much.*

The receptionist has her back turned to him, so he reaches up, removes the flyer, and stuffs it in his pocket.

On the drive home, the dog rests on a blanket in the back seat. Karns stops for take-out pizza at Luigi's. Linda, who works the drive-thru window, hands him the pizza box, along with a small sack of red pepper flakes and parmesan. Her nails are painted a vibrant green. "Treat for Mitzi is in the bag, too," she says. "See you next time," then she slides the window closed.

Back at his apartment, he gives the dog the milk bone treat and a fresh bowl of water. He eats four slices of pizza at the kitchen table while the dog, in her new cast, this time wrapped in a pink bandage, waits for her share of the crust. He thinks, *What's the harm?* and tosses her a piece of it, which she catches and chews.

He gathers up the couch stuffing in a trash bag, tries cleaning the carpet with dish soap and a sponge, but realizes it won't come clean. He'll have to rent a cleaner from the grocery store.

He carries her to the bedroom and puts her in her dog bed in the corner. When he comes out of the shower, she is asleep, so he sits on the edge of his bed and watches her. She lets out a few muffled sleep barks. Karns sees her legs twitch as if she is dreaming of running. The vet said another two months, then the cast could come off. When he asked if she would walk with a limp, Dr. Wallace said no, that she would be good as new, as if nothing had ever happened.

He picks up the crumpled flyer from the nightstand and looks closely at the photo. There are some slight differences, he thinks. The dog in the photo looks a bit furrier, though it might have been a photo taken in winter. The ears are a perfect match, but lots of dogs have similar ears, and the silver patch on the chest seems slightly more slanted and wider than Mitzi's.

Even if it turned out Mitzi is a lost member of the Davis family, he decides it would be unkind to show up with the dog in such rough shape. Too much to explain. And he has at least another two months before the cast comes off—plenty of time for him to think things through, and even then, she might need more recovery time. And frankly, she didn't seem to miss them much, any more than the human Mitzi misses him, living in the high mountains, in the good company of her sister, Angel.

Besides, he figures the Davis's have likely given up hope of ever finding her by now. He is sure they've already stopped circling the neighborhood looking for her, or putting up more *Lost Dog* flyers, or running ads in the local paper. Soon, if it hadn't happened already, the dog toys would be dumped in a box in the garage, half-empty bag of dog food shoved to the back of the pantry, water bowls put away. It is entirely likely they have stopped talking about the dog at all by now. People get over those things with time. Dogs disappear every day. Shelters are full of them. He figures there is a better than even chance they've already adopted another dog anyway, and given it a good name.

It is late. He pulls down the comforter and sheet, adjusts his pillow, slides into bed, reaches over to turn off the light.

He hears the wind blowing outside. Headlights sweep across his walls. Someone pulls into a parking space out front. He hears the sound of a car door. He thinks again of asking to move to a second-floor apartment when his lease is up. Maybe even a two-bedroom place, although he can't think of a specific use for a second bedroom, other than to have more space to just walk around in.

If they hadn't signed a lease agreement for their house, and if a family hadn't moved in, he might have considered moving back himself. But Mitzi already sent him a fairly substantial check, and he had to admit it made living on a teacher's salary much easier. She included a postcard with the check—a *Welcome to the Land of Enchantment* postcard, featuring five colorful kachina dolls. She didn't write anything on the postcard, or add a note with the check itself. It could just as well have been sent to anybody.

Karns sees a flash of lightning, hears a distant rumble of thunder, and another gust of wind. The dog whines in the corner. It is pitch-dark in the room. "You're all right, girl," he says. Another clap of thunder moves through the room, this time loud enough to rattle the windows. The storm is moving closer. She whines again. He reaches over to turn the lamp on, thinking the light might comfort her, but pauses before turning the switch. "Maggie?" he says into the darkness just when the next roll of thunder begins to sound, but not so loudly he can't hear the rhythmic beat of her tail thumping against the wall.

He waits until seven a.m. before he calls Mitzi. It's six a.m. in her time zone, and she doesn't answer on his first try. It goes to voicemail, so he hangs up, then calls again. He's driving.

"Is something wrong?" she says.

"No, not really."

"Are you sick?"

"Why would you assume I'm sick?" He hears her yawn. He's not sure if it's a real yawn or a manufactured one.

"What time is it anyway?"

"Pretty early."

"Did you forget about the time difference?"

"No," he says. "I thought about it before I called. It's only an hour's difference, though. If I was calling from London, which is actually tomorrow, it would be like 1:00 a.m. your time." Karns isn't sure he has the math right, but he says, "So you should probably thank me."

"You aren't calling from London are you? Are you in some sort of trouble?"

"I'm not sick or in London."

"Trouble then?"

"I just needed to ask you something, and I figured I'd clear the hurdle now while the day is new."

"What hurdle?" Then she pauses and asks, "Did you meet someone? Is that what this is about?"

"No," Karns says, although the slight alarm he detects in her voice gives him some pleasure. "Nothing like that. I just wanted to ask if I might move back into the house. Once their lease is up, of course. I'm stuck for the next six months in my place anyway."

She doesn't answer right away. "Why would you want to do that?"

"For the extra space."

"Do you mean just more space, or that particular space?"

"Both," he answers. It's early on Saturday, so the traffic is light. He drives under the speed limit.

"What's happened?"

"Why should I need something to happen to want to live in my own house?" He hears her sigh, then the muffle of moving her phone to the other ear. He imagines she is sitting up in bed, her hair tied up in a ragged topknot like she always has it when she goes to bed.

"That might be complicated," she finally says. "Financially, I mean. Maybe legally. I'm not sure."

Karns turns into a neighborhood. The houses are not large, but all of them are neat, the lawns mown, the driveways and curbs trimmed and swept. The streets are still wet from the rain. "I'll pay you rent," he says. "Whatever the current tenants pay."

He expects her to ask if he's won the lottery, or taken on a second job, but she doesn't. "And what about the family that just moved in?"

He is looking for an address. "Leases expire. When you rent that's part of the deal. A temporary situation, right? You go in expecting time to run out. Tick-tock, tick-tock."

She is silent again, then says, "Are you feeling morose today? Is today one of those days for you?"

"Not that I've noticed."

"Are you driving around like you do when you feel morose?"

"That's your word of the day, is it?"

"Can I ask you something?" she says. He thinks she is going to ask again if there is someone else but she doesn't. "What's the point of trying to return to what isn't anymore?"

Karns pulls into a short, steep driveway. There is a bicycle on the porch, a few yellow marigolds in clay pots, a couple of white rocking chairs. He shuts off the car's engine. "I miss having a backyard," he says. "I want a backyard."

"For barbeques? That sort of thing? Parties for work friends? You have met someone, haven't you."

He checks the house address he wrote on a scrap of paper. "I want a dog," he says. "It's for the dog I'm going to get."

Mitzi says, "What brought this on?"

A woman opens the front door of the house. She is middle-aged, perhaps younger than Karns, maybe much younger. She stands behind the glass storm door, then steps to the porch, followed by a boy wearing a green baseball cap who ducks under her arm. Karns lifts his hand from the steering wheel and waves. He asks Mitzi to hold on.

The woman on the porch waves back. Karns turns to the dog in the back seat. She slept most of the drive, but now she lifts her head and stands up crookedly, still managing the new cast.

"Mitz?"

"I'm still here," she says.

"Give me few minutes, or we can just hang up and talk later if you want." The boy has come down from the porch. He is wearing orange flip-flops too short for his feet. He stops at the back window of the car, cups his hands to see inside, then shouts something to his mother. The woman puts her hand over her mouth.

"Sure," Mitzi says.

The boy opens the car door. When he hesitates, Karns says, "Go ahead, then."

The woman steps off the porch, walks to the driveway to stand at the driver's window. Her arms are crossed against the morning chill. She has a hummingbird tattoo on one forearm, her dark hair drawn into a high ponytail. She is dressed for the gym.

The night before, right after he made the call to the Davis's, he practiced things to say, but suddenly forgets what any of them were. On the phone he told her about the accident, and about seeing the *Lost*

Dog notice. He told her he is a science teacher at Remington High School, which he immediately regretted, then he apologized for calling so late. She started crying, her voice breaking, and when she stopped, she said she would give him the reward money, plus cover all the medical expenses, but he said there was no need. He told her about the appointment with the vet, for when the cast should come off. He told her it was all covered, that it was the least he could do, without more explanation. They agreed to the early morning meeting.

Now she stands at his door and taps the glass. Karns feels his heart beating. He wishes he had smoked a joint before he left his apartment. He wishes he had waited at least a few more days before he called, or just left things as they were. He thinks, just put the car in reverse and go home. The whole thing is a mistake, one big huge bungle. But then he hears the boy kick the rear car door closed and sees him hurry toward the house with the dog held tight against his chest, her head bobbing up and down with each step.

The mother is saying his name loud enough for him to hear through the glass. "Mr. Karns?" she says. She is smiling. He finds the power button and when the window is fully down she quickly reaches through the opening. He takes her hand in his. Her fingers are thin and cold. Before she lets go, Mitzi's voice comes from the phone he's dropped to his lap. "Hello? So do I hang up first, or you?"

Glow

Murtry was trying to kill the big Labrador with his bare hands because the dog made the mistake of growling at his food bowl, but he couldn't find a weak spot in the dog's barrel neck. First he crow-barred with his forearm under the Lab's jaw, his other hand in a tight fist pressing just above the shoulder blades. When that didn't yield the crack of death, he held the squalling animal's melon head in both hands and torqued the spine at the base of its skull, like trying to unscrew a stubborn cap from a gas pipe.

Lorna, on the porch, her eyes half-closed in a wince, sat in Buster's lap, virtually burying him in his wheelchair. She was trying not to appear too concerned by the yelps, at the spectacle of her father straddling the writhing black mass of dog. She knew Buster was feeling weak, his lung sacs full of the phlegm she hadn't drummed out. His hand rested on her bare thigh, fingers tucked under the hem of her pink cotton shorts, and every time her father changed position over the dog, Buster slid his fingers a little further along the curve of her leg, cradling her like a baby on his shallow lap, until she felt his palm pressing into the flesh of her hip.

"Give me the strength of Samson, sweet Jesus," Murtry said, his voiced pitched by exertion, to which Buster, his own voiced strained by the weight of the woman on his lap, squeaked in answer: "Yes, Lord, yes."

The dog's tongue was pinched between his teeth, a flattened piece of pink bubble gum, and Lorna, who was the first to see the blood between her father's fingers, forgot about Buster's roaming hand and said, "That's enough."

But Murtry was already at a standstill after trying every angle of torment, so he finally took a step back and kicked the dog in the belly. Rather than running, the Lab rolled onto his side, blowing hard, his jowls flubbering.

"I suppose," Buster said, quickly skimming his hand back to Lorna's knee, "you could just shoot him and save yourself some sweat." He coughed out the last words, grumbled deep in his chest to clear his airways.

"Leave him alone," Lorna said. "He'll do no such thing." She watched the Lab struggle into a sitting position, hind legs quivering under the weight of his enormous body. "That poor old dog is likely to die as it is from all that wrestling."

Murtry wiped his hands on his thighs, painted little streaks of red on his ginger pants. "One of us is bleeding," he said, examined his palms and thick knuckles for cuts, then leaned over to peer at the panting dog. "Tongue's bit," then he gave the dog a quick scratch behind a ragged ear and a broad, gentle stroke on the bowl of his skull. "He'll live."

Murtry was like a thunderstorm, Lorna thought, a sudden squall of chaos, but tender in passing. He treated people the same way. When Buster rolled down the road from the church with her perched for the first time in his lap, coming home from a revival meeting Buster preached, Murtry threatened to wheel him into the murky water of the baptismal pond. Now Buster was his favorite, and he called him Son even though the wedding was still seven months away.

Buster, of course, believed Murtry was a blessed man, spent long hours at the kitchen table with him studying the Gospels over coffee and lemon bundt cake, the pair of them breaking into prayers of thanksgiving for the rain, for the punishment of drought, for the crippling grip of cold, for the health of Murtry's laying hens. "You know what Murtry did today?" he said to her once, lingering in the passenger seat of his green Pontiac before they went into Margie's Restaurant for spicy barbecue and mustardy potato salad. "He recited the books of the Bible backwards. Revelation to Genesis. Not many men can do that. Not many literally know the Good Book frontways and backways."

"That's his trick," Lorna said, dusting her face with powder in the rearview mirror. "It's the only one he knows."

Murtry plodded off to the barn, legs wobbling like a drunk leaving a bar fight.

The Lab belly-crawled under the porch steps and whined himself to sleep.

Lorna waited for the sun to burn itself free from the woods across the road, then pushed Buster through the front door and into Murtry's bedroom. She hoisted him out of his chair, sliding her arms under his and giving him a bear hug, her chin braced against his shoulder. What little help his legs could give was just enough to get him sprawled face down on the large quilted bed. She went to the linen closet and brought back a thick blue towel, wedged it under his chin to catch the globbies, then lay down beside him and began thumping his back with an open palm.

"Any requests?"

"*The Old Rugged Cross*, then *Amazing Grace*. But not too fast."

Lorna sang, clubbing Buster's back to the rhythm.

Before she made it to the second verse, Buster coughed up a yellow worm of phlegm onto the towel, then wiped his slick chin with the back of his hand. Lorna slapped for more, moving her hand from the small of his back to the hard cable of spine between his shoulder blades, coaxing the mucus up like she was squeezing toothpaste. "I talked to Betty Anne yesterday about going to the Holy Land. You know what she said? She said we may as well make a bed on the church pew as go to the Holy Land for a honeymoon. Of course, I told her I always wanted to walk the road to Damascus, at least part way, and set my bare feet on the stones where Apostle Paul was struck blind by the Lord." Lorna hummed *Amazing Grace*, careful not to let the tempo get away from her while she watched Buster's back heave with coughs that failed to produce anything. "Betty Anne says we ought to go to Kansas City or New Orleans or Dallas. She's says there's no restaurants in the Holy Land, which I suspect is not true, although I can't imagine what kind there'd be."

Buster grunted, cleared his vocal cords of stickiness, said, "It's best to forget what Betty Anne says and stick what the Lord says. 'I will come like a thief in the night. Be ye vigilant and ever watchful.'"

"That's true," Lorna mumbled. "We must be ready in the twinkling of an eye," although the thought of The Second Coming happening during her honeymoon struck her as terribly poor timing. She pushed the idea from her mind and concentrated on gathering up the final beautiful notes of *Amazing Grace*.

Buster rolled over on his back, smacked his lips, took in deep draughts of air. He closed his eyes while Lorna gently wiped his face with a wadded Kleenex.

"Hon?"

"Yeah?"

"Where *do* you eat in the Holy Land?"

Buster stayed in the house, watched wrestling on the small TV in the kitchen while Lorna helped Murtry clean the chicken house. She wore knee high rubber boots and leather gloves, scooped up knots of dirty hay from the laying boxes and tossed it into a wheelbarrow. The air swirled with dust and Lorna tied a red bandanna over her mouth to stave off the pungent ammonia of droppings.

Murtry broke open a ragged bale of hay and handed wedges to Lorna, who carefully lined the laying boxes, shaping the hay into comfortable bowls, even though she knew the hens would scratch them out on their own.

They, of course, wouldn't have any children, she thought. Buster wasn't up to that. But kids weren't mandatory. And besides, Buster was good with his hands, and sometimes she considered it was better that way because he had to pay attention to her and listen to what she told him, like giving him lessons on the piano. There was the weekend Murtry went to visit his sister in Gulfport, and her and Buster spent the whole night on the divan, and before they were through Buster was crying and using his hands and telling Lorna one minute how beautiful she was and the next minute saying how sorry he was for being so sick and weak. She snapped at him, told him to concentrate, and he stopped crying and got that determined look on his face, tongue sticking out like a little kid trying to trace out his first letters.

And Buster was often filled with the spirit and liked to hold her close and whisper in her ear while his thin fingers roamed over her. Now, every time Buster preached in church and the sweat poured across his red face and he swiped a clean white handkerchief over his forehead and cheeks and mouth Lorna couldn't sit still in the pew for thinking about him and his hands. Sometimes she had to thumb through a hymnal and try not to look at him while he was proclaiming the Gospel, and her sitting next to Sister Bernice Lange.

There was a man before Buster, and she started thinking about him while Murtry wheeled the first load of smelly hay to the bar ditch across the pasture. She was nineteen. He was a long-haul trucker named Larry Burdette, and he took her fifty miles from home and gave her an amethyst necklace he kept in an empty saltine box under the seat. She remembered his aftershave, which smelled like celery, and him being on top of her with the gear shift poking into her ribs and the rumble of the idling diesel engine beneath them. And she wondered why he didn't cut the engine but let it churn on and on, like they were caught in the belly of some snoring monster that might wake up at any second and roar down the highway of its own accord.

He said he was going to take her to Abilene and buy her a thirty ounce beef steak and wash it down with cold beer, and then they were going to set out cross-country and live it up on the road, free as birds. He poured Tequila from a green Stanley thermos into Dixie cups and they sang Waylon Jennings songs until midnight.

Lorna got out to pee behind a patch of dry mesquite and when she climbed back into the cab, Larry was singing *Luckinbach, Texas* and crying with his head down, his thick, tattoed arms hanging over the steering wheel. He told Lorna he had a little girl in Beaumont he hadn't seen in more than a year, and she had a twisted foot and wore a special shoe. He said he was trying to get up enough nerve to visit, and he bought the amethyst necklace from a roadside stand in Arizona for her but decided it wasn't quite right and he couldn't go on to Beaumont until he found a precious gift to make her happy.

Larry eventually fell asleep slumped over the wheel and she was left alone to watched a storm rise in the west and sweep toward them. The truck shook against the wind gusts and the rain drummed so hard on the roof she couldn't hear herself think.

Later she woke up from her own fitful sleep with an ache between her legs. She crawled from the cab into the wet darkness and caught a ride with an onion truck driven by a quiet Mexican woman on her way to Lufkin. She called Betty Anne from a Texaco.

Betty Anne pulled up two hours later, and by the look of her red, swollen eyes, Lorna thought she must have been crying from worry the entire trip, but they weren't in the car more than five minutes when Betty Anne started laughing. She told Lorna she was fit to bust and was awfully sorry for making fun but she'd already been at it for an hour and just couldn't make herself stop.

And Lorna, who had stood tearfully in the dark trying to convince herself that Larry Burdette had virtually cast a spell of evil on her and ruined her for life, found herself laughing right along with her and they had to pull off the highway and lean on their knees.

It was a shameful episode, she thought, handing Murtry a rake so he could clean out the corners. Here she was, working beside her own daddy and Buster watching wrestling on television in the kitchen, and her with the memory of something like that rattling around in her head. What worried her the most, though, was the notion of walking down the aisle with Buster, on the happiest and holiest day of her life, and knowing that what she was going to be hearing, no matter how much she tried to smother it under the organ music, was that diesel engine rolling under her like the voice of Lucifer himself, muttering in some mysterious tongue.

One of the hens, an old, gray Barred Rock, came clucking into the chicken house as if to inspect the work. Lorna touched its rump with the toe of her boot, and the hen launched herself with ragged beats of her short wings into one of the nesting boxes. Murtry, busy scattering hay on the floor, eyed the bird with cold suspicion. "She's bluffing," he said. "That's one ready for the soup pot."

The hen, her scaly legs pale from age, staggered around the boxes from one to another, until finally settling into a corner. She scratched deep into the hay until she clawed at wood.

"Give her a minute. It's a wonder every animal on the place isn't boiling on the stove by sundown, including that dog."

Murtry grumbled to himself and walked off to the barn for another half-bale. Lorna sat on a plastic feed bucket and absently picked at the chaff clinging to her shirt while she watched the hen stiffen, as if it were turning to stone.

When she was a little girl she spent hours in the cool calm of the chicken house, eyeing the nervous hens as they wandered in one at time to lay. First, they fussed about the boxes, sometimes scratched out a nest only to move to the next one and start all over again. Once they settled, there was that blank stare that turned their yellow eyes to glass, a concentration so intense that when they were through you would think they had solved the all the world's problems just by laying an egg.

She waited on the hen, through Murtry's bustling in and out.

She waited until the corner she sat in was covered in shadow.

The hen stood up occasionally, preened the striped feathers that hung ragged on her crop, looked sideways at the woman resting quietly below, then settled gently into the nest again, as if the air were let out of her.

After a few hours, Murtry peeked inside, said Buster was starting to wheeze.

"I'll be along," Lorna said, but she didn't move from her perch on the bucket.

The hen dozed, strained, dozed.

Lorna squirmed uncomfortably.

Another hen, a metallic red and black Bantam no bigger than Lorna's foot, hurriedly flew into a nest, deposited a small brownish egg in a matter of minutes, then scurried out again.

"See there," Lorna said, "that's how you do it," coaxing it like a midwife, making herself good company.

She dozed herself, arms folded tightly across her chest, thought about Murtry wrestling with the dog, trying to break his neck for nothing more than a little growl; and she thought about the quilt she was making for Buster's mother, and how it had five stars and two quarter-moons and a blue planet she didn't know the name of; she thought about the wedding and the two dresses at Dillard's to decide between and what she would wear on the plane afterwards and the honeymoon on the other side of the world.

She would rather go to New Orleans or Dallas, or even Shreveport, where she was sure there were restaurants a person would actually want to eat it after getting married. Besides, she couldn't very well wheel Buster down the road to Damascus by herself, and because he wouldn't want to be left behind she probably wouldn't go either. They would stay in the hotel (she imagined dirt floors with camels plunging their noses through the open windows), order figs and unleavened bread and hope to have a few cubes of ice in glasses of sweet tea, and Buster would eventually get the urge and she would lay back on a lumpy straw mattress and try to enjoy herself and close her eyes so she wouldn't see his tongue sticking out. Afterwards he would use the color maps in his bible to point out how far they were from the actual Mount of Olives and the actual hill of Golgatha and the actual tomb where the stone rolled away.

She finally admitted she couldn't stand the thought of any of it, but Buster was set on making the trip, and the church had even taken up a special collection for them to pay for plane tickets, and the Sunday before the wedding there was to be a prayer service to ask the Lord to heal Buster of his afflictions and fill him so full of the Holy Spirit that they all might be nourished for years to come. But, she thought, what if the spirit of Jesus was still there, walking the dusty streets of Jerusalem like some ghost that wouldn't leave the house it died in? Couldn't He poke His nose in the hotel window just as well as a camel?

Sister Bernice Lange, with tall purple hair and a vast collection of nylon scarves to keep it up, had pulled Lorna aside one Wednesday night and said Lorna, too, was in for a wealth of blessing for showing kindness and mercy to the lame, offering herself as a loving handmaiden and all-around vessel to a minister of the Kingdom of God. "Whatever you do to a least brother of mine," Sister Bernice said, squinting her eyes to help her remember the scripture, "you do for me."

She had never considered Buster the least of anyone, and she suspected Sister Bernice was hinting at more than just helping a pastor get around and clearing his lungs. She liked the word "handmaiden" though, the quiet sound of it in her head, even though she didn't care for Sister Lange, and likely the whole congregation, pondering over her sacrifices.

No, she didn't like the thought of any of it.

The hen let out a low whistle, like someone signaling from the opposite shore of a narrow lake, then stood up and clumsily dropped an egg, a perfectly round and off-white egg no bigger than a Ping-Pong ball.

Lorna nudged the hen aside and stared into the nest. It looked like an oversized pearl, with a nearly translucent shell, so delicate she feared it might crumble if she stared too hard.

She had seen eggs like it before. Murtry called them "chunkers," because all they were good for was to throw out into the pasture. It was the kind of malformed egg old hens bordering on uselessness laid.

Lorna gently scooped it up and carried it out of the hen house. She half-expected it to disappear in her hand, melt away like a hailstone, so she hurried down the path toward the house, her rubber boots flopping like thick waves against her shins.

Murtry called to her from the entrance of the barn, but she didn't dare take her eyes off the object in her hand, for as it dried it turned whiter and seemed to glow in her palm, as if it had a warming bulb inside.

She called out to Buster to come to the porch to see something. She listened for the screen door, the sound of wheels on gritty wood. She strained to keep her eyes fixed on the cooling egg. It wavered in her hand, a liquid white that threatened to slip through her fingers and seep into the grass.

She heard Buster on the porch above her, heard the hard, rattling breaths he always made when he needed tending to. He coughed roughly and spat and the phlegm landing like yellow glue on the step just above her.

"I've been waiting a long time," he said. "You're way past time, hon." His voice was grating, the sound climbing from deep within the cavern of his chest like it did when he preached a long sermon on the wretchedness of sin. He would wheel himself around the altar, glaring at every face in the congregation sucking in gasps of air as if he were drawing all the evil of the world into his lungs.

She felt a slight flush of heat rise in her face and decided she could not look at him. Instead she focussed on the curious, delicate egg she cradled in her palm. If she were to turn away for a second, it might burst into a shining bird that would shoot straight into the sky, and she would miss it all together.

Then she thought of Larry Burdette again, crying over his little girl with the twisted foot and realized what she held was the perfect gift, and Larry would spend a lifetime looking for what she cradled in her palm and never find it. What a lame girl in Beaumont would do with such an egg, she didn't know, but she could hold it up to the light and look at it.

And she remembered draping the amethyst necklace around the radio knob just before slipping from the truck cab that night. She was sure it was still dangling there, undelivered, left behind by a woman who's name he couldn't remember, swaying with every turn in the road like some heavy chain around the man's heart.

Murtry said, "What's that she got?"

"Lord if I know," Buster said.

Lorna felt them closing in around her, the liquid gurgle of Buster's breathing, the heavy tread of Murtry's boots. She took a few steps back and gently cupped her other hand over the egg, shielding it from their stares.

I'm in Garrison, Texas

Cousin DeeRay passed away at the age of forty-three from heart failure brought on by drugs. He was found by some kids on the bank of a farm pond. That's the story I heard, at least. He had already been dead for a few years by the time I even heard about it from Nan, DeeRay's half-sister who lived in South Dakota. She called out of the blue to talk to me. I asked Nan if she was married and had kids and she said yes, two of each. I wasn't sure if she meant two marriages or kids, or both, but I let it go. I also asked if DeeRay had been married and had kids, and she said he married a woman named Vanessa, and there were kids. How many she didn't know. They hadn't talked in years, any more than she and I had.

Nan and I promised to meet up somewhere in Kansas for dinner with our two families—which I knew would never happen—and she gave me Vanessa's phone number. It was after ten o'clock at night, but I called anyway.

"Hello?" I said. "Is this Vanessa?"

"Who's calling?"

"Sorry to bother you," I said, "but I just found out about DeeRay. I'm his cousin, Bill. I live in Oklahoma."

"Who's this?" she asked. She sounded sleepy.

"Bill," I said. "Cousin DeeRay's cousin."

There was a long pause, which might have given her time to compose herself, to fight back the tears on being reminded out of the blue by a complete stranger that her husband was still dead. But she said, "He never mentioned you."

"Really?" I said. "That's strange. We were pals." I didn't tell her I hadn't talked to DeeRay in decades, but I did tell her how I found out. "Nan told me what happened," I said, then, after a long silence, "You still there?"

I heard nothing. Then she hung up.

I told my wife I needed to take a trip to Garrison, Texas, to visit a long-lost cousin whose wife had contacted me out of the blue and invited me for a visit. I teach English at our local community college, and Spring Break was coming up. My wife still had work, so we hadn't made any plans: just TV and yard work, and a movie with the in-laws, which didn't interest me in the least.

"I didn't know you had any cousins."

"Just the one," I said, which was the truth. I was sitting at the kitchen table drinking a cup of coffee. She was mashing big russets in a green glass bowl with a wire masher.

"Really," she said, not as a question, but more like a doubtful retort. She's a master at doubtful retorts.

"Just the one," I said again. "Here's the thing, though. He's dead."

"Really. From what?"

"Plane crash," I said, just for the hell of it. "It made the news last year, only I didn't know I had any connection to the victims. Icy runway, I believe."

"I think I heard about that," she said.

"Sure you did," I said. "It was all over everywhere."

She put the green bowl of mostly mashed potatoes into the microwave but didn't set the timer or turn it on. "Do you want me to go?"

I said, "Not unless you just want to."

"I would have nothing to do there. What do you do in Garrison, Texas?" She set the timer and started the microwave and the bowl of mashed potatoes spun slowly behind the glass door.

"Visit graves," I said. "Unless there's a zoo."

I remember climbing rough cedar trees with him and eating melting popsicles in the summer heat. I remember he had a little dog named Honey. When I thought of Cousin DeeRay, I saw myself as a ten-year-old running barefoot with a half-flat Wilson football down Mims Road, DeeRay playing defense after he kicked me the ball, coming straight at me with his thick arms spread wide. When he got his hands on you, and set his feet, there was no way around or through him. If things had gone differently in his life, he might have been a professional football player, or a WWF star.

DeeRay's mother ran off when he was only fourteen. She eventually surfaced in South Dakota, married to an iron worker named Antonio. That's how half-sister Nan came into the world. Before his mother left, DeeRay's dad, my dad's brother, went to prison for molesting a kid at vacation bible school. He died in Huntsville Penitentiary a year later from lung cancer.

After that, DeeRay lived in Lufkin with a foster family for a while. They already had four kids of their own, but all old enough to be out of the house most of the time, so I never met any of them. DeeRay's foster dad, Gary, took us fishing in a tricked-out Ranger bass boat one summer. He bought us each a new rod and reel, and we shared a new tackle box that held hooks and bobbers and lead weights, along with a few lures. One lure was a rubber frog with a hook hidden in its back. When I asked Gary what kind of fish ate frogs, he said, "Sharks," and then he winked at me. Gary was a big winker.

The thing I remember most from that trip, though, other than the frog lure, was that when DeeRay tried to make a cast, Gary told him he needed a better follow-through if he expected to get the spinner bait more than three feet from the bow of the boat. DeeRay complained the lure was too light, so Gary took the rod and reel and spinner and made a perfect long cast, dropping the lure right beside a tangle of partially submerged tree branches. After a couple more equally perfect casts, he hooked a nice Crappie, but instead of taking it off the hook and dropping it in the tank, he just held it in the air, so close to DeeRay's face that when the fish flipped its tail it knocked off DeeRay's new sunglasses, which bounced along the edge of the boat then fell into the lake. Gary laughed, so DeeRay broke his new rod across his knee and threw it into the water. Then he picked up the tackle box and tossed in into the lake as well. I heard the rattle of all the hooks and weights and lures as it flew through the air, then came the big splash.

Gary just stared at the water for a minute, then said, "That'll do," and he sat down at the boat's steering wheel and muttered to himself for a while. Then he told me to bring in my line. He took off his ball cap, ran his fingers through his thinning hair, then put the cap back on. He did that three times before he finally fired up the engine and took us to the dock. DeeRay and I sat in the back seat of Gary's pickup while Gary loaded the boat on the trailer, locked the motor, pulled the hull tight with the winch. No one said anything on the drive home, but I remember looking over at Cousin DeeRay and saw he was smiling. I didn't ask him about what.

After that, DeeRay went to live with our old granddad for a couple of years. When he turned eighteen, he moved out.

The last time I saw DeeRay was the summer we were just old enough to drive and we took our granddad's white Chevy Nova for a spin around a dimly lit Nacogdoches, Texas. DeeRay asked me if I was good with my dukes in case we ran into trouble and I lied that I was good in a pinch, although I had never been in a real fight in my life, except with a big sixth-grade girl name Tammy Dunkel, who roughed me up pretty good.

We pulled into a gas station later that night and I went inside and bought two cans of soda and paid for the gas. When I came out,

DeeRay was standing beside his car with a kid in a headlock. There was another kid there as well, about our age, too, but he just sat in his car with the driver's door open and yelled, "Shake loose, Butch!"

The kid in the headlock never made a sound even though his mouth was moving. His face was red. I didn't know who I was supposed to help, or even if I could, but eventually I realized the kid named Butch was starting to droop in the shoulders and his knees were giving way. I don't remember exactly what I said to Cousin DeeRay, but I do know I had to get right in his face to say it. When he finally let go, the kid fell backwards and landed on the concrete. His friend got out and helped him up and guided him back to their car, which belched blue smoke on its way out of the lot.

On the way home I asked DeeRay if he knew those guys, and he said he'd never seen them before in his life. I asked him if the kid named Butch did something to him, and he said they just looked like they might be from out of town, maybe Tyler, maybe even Houston. Then he said, "You just can't ever be too careful around some people," and he smiled, and hit the gas hard.

I always knew he could handle himself, but even after that night, even after seeing Butch with his head held so tight between DeeRay's forearm and bicep that he couldn't breathe, my cousin always seemed more clown than bruiser, someone who liked to show what he could do if he wanted to, but didn't need to actually do it. An oaf, of sorts. I couldn't imagine him busting a nose or breaking a jaw. I suppose that's why he didn't die in a bar fight, or end up in prison. All I knew was that he died fishing at a farm pond. Maybe his heart just gave out from the drugs, or maybe just because he was having a such good time at a favorite fishing hole. That's how people go sometimes, too. A sudden jolt of contentment.

For the trip south, I decided to go old school, so I dug out my AAA Road Atlas and worked on a route to Garrison: I-35 South through Oklahoma City, then to Dallas/Ft. Worth, then a jog east toward Shreveport, then south again just before I hit the Louisiana state line. It measured out to be over five hundred miles, which would put it at around eight hours of drive time, but I decided not to take the whole chunk at once.

I packed a few changes of clothes, said goodbye to my wife, who didn't seem too disappointed at my leaving for a few days, gassed up my car, bought a big soda, some cheddar crackers, a couple of apple fruit pies, and hit the road right after breakfast.

Once I was on Interstate 35 and made it outside Oklahoma City, I drove holding the atlas against the steering wheel for a while, charted a path through some of the smaller towns. I would go through Palestine and Tucker, then south to Slocum, east to Alto, then north through Nacogdoches, and on to Garrison.

I stopped just short of Ft. Worth and had a chicken finger basket and vanilla malt at a run-down DQ. The place was virtually empty since it was well past lunchtime. A kid with a runny nose sat with his mother in a booth and picked at his hamburger with his drinking straw. A pale-skinned woman in a hairnet wiped tables and repositioned salt and pepper shakers and napkin holders while I ate slowly and pulled hard on the straw against the thickness of the shake.

I had a one-night reservation at a motel called the Traveler's Friend outside Tyler, and hit town late, at around 11:00 p.m. The motel didn't have a restaurant but down the street within walking distance was a 24-hour truck stop diner, so I checked into my room, unloaded my one piece of luggage, washed my hands and face and neck, took a cherry cigarillo from the box of eight I bought at a gas stop on a whim, lit it, and smoked my way down the quiet road. By the time I was at the front door of the truck stop I was light-headed and a little nauseous from the sweet cigar (I'm not a smoker), but I made it into a booth just inside the door, took some deep breaths, and felt better.

The waitress, a girl who couldn't have been a minute more than sixteen, peach-colored hair parted down the middle and hanging limp over her shoulders, took my order: two eggs sunny side up, bacon, toast, a glass of whole milk and coffee. It was the kind of meal my wife would never cook—breakfast for a late-night dinner—so I dove in and ordered another slice of toast for sopping. I was on my second cup of coffee when a man walked in with a towel folded in his hands and a bottle of shampoo and an unwrapped bar of soap. His shirttail hung out of his wrinkled corduroy pants and his face was rough with whiskers.

"Hey, Princess," he said to the waitress, who was sitting at the cash register and reading a magazine.

"Hi, Ray," she said. "Shower's open. Help yourself," and the man walked past me and down a yellow hallway.

I decided I needed a piece of pecan pie, which I could see they had on an old-fashioned pie carousel, so I said, "Hey, Princess, can you bring me a piece of that pecan pie with a scoop of vanilla?"

She looked up from her magazine, her face blank, then she closed the magazine and rose listlessly from the chair. She opened the carousel and took out a slice of pie on a saucer and went into the kitchen. In a minute she came back with the pie and a big scoop of half-melted chocolate ice cream on top.

"Thanks," I said, "but I wanted vanilla."

She sat back down to her magazine and said, without looking up, "Seems we just ran out of vanilla, Sir. Just this very second."

I figured it must have been the "Princess" that got me chocolate. I ate the pie and ice cream and left her a decent tip.

Back at the motel room I watched some TV and then took a shower. I called my wife and gave her the room number for some reason, just in case.

"How's your trip so far?" she asked.

"Fine," I said. "I think I'm going to write a travel piece about diners. You know, the lousy food and colorful characters sort of thing? I've already jotted down some ideas."

"That's nice. You haven't written much lately. That sounds like a nice topic for you." I heard our TV going in the background. I couldn't figure out what she was watching though and didn't ask.

She was spot on about my writing. The last publication I had was a five-hundred-word book review, which doesn't move you much closer to getting tenure. Before that, it had been four years since I'd published anything.

"Have a good night then," she said. "Call me tomorrow?"

"I will," I said, and hung up.

My stomach was full and grumbled under the weight of my late, heavy meal so I turned in halfway through a pretty decent movie. At 2:00 a.m. I woke up sick, so I got a wet washrag and stayed awake in bed until around 5:00 a.m. When I felt well enough to travel again, I walked to the front desk and checked out. I had planned on another meal at a Denny's I passed on the way in, a short stack of pancakes and pork sausage and orange juice and coffee, but I couldn't stomach the thought of it, so I left Tyler behind and drank bottled water until I felt settled enough even to drive the speed limit.

Mid-morning I stopped at a roadside park and sat at a concrete picnic table and ate the last package of my cheese crackers in a final test of my stomach before I hunted up some real lunch when I made it to Garrison. The pine trees grew tall around the park and the ground was covered in brown needles. There were squirrels and birds, and I watched a tall man in khaki shorts haul a green ice chest from the trunk of his car and sit at one of the other picnic tables. He was eventually joined by a tall, thin woman and two girls. They made sandwiches and ate chips off paper plates and drank sodas. They looked like vacationers—sunglasses, comfortable sandals and sneakers, loose Tshirts, had the air of folks who were in no particular hurry to be anywhere. They had a little black Weiner dog that systematically peed on a half-dozen trees and then got two of my tires. The woman wore a white visor, and both girls had on matching blue plastic sunglasses shaped like dolphins.

I almost wished I had asked my wife to come along, but thought, who was I kidding? She would have hated the truck stop and Princess and the motel and the concrete bench I sat on. She preferred posher digs and much healthier food. And she couldn't eat comfortably outside for fear of insects. I got over my homesickness pretty quick and left the park.

It only took another two hours from the roadside park to the city limits of Garrison. The highway I was on turned into Main Street and soon I was downtown, passing by small shops and insurance agencies and hardware stores. I saw a sign for Mike's Burgers, and parked. Inside, a fat man wearing a paper hat and a white, greasy apron worked a grill behind the counter, like something you would see in an old movie. I took a stool at the counter and a waitress in a sleeveless black shirt and plaid pants came over to take my order. Her arms were brown and traced by thin, white scars.

"You want the special?" she asked before I had a chance to say anything.

"What's the special?"

"Onion and jalapeño burger with salsa and a side of spicy fries."

"Does that come with an ambulance?" I joked, and she smiled a polite smile. "I'll just have a cheeseburger and a side salad."

"We don't got salads," she said, "except macaroni salad. You want macaroni salad?"

"Just the burger and some fries, then," I said, "and a glass of milk, unless you have beer."

"We got Coors and Bud."

"Is it cold?"

She looked over her shoulder as if I had been speaking to someone behind her, then looked back at me. "It's in the fridge," she said. "It's bound to be cold."

"I'll take a Bud, then."

"You still want the milk?"

"Just the beer and a glass of ice water with a slice of lime."

"We got lemons," she said.

"Then a beer with water and a slice of lemon."

She scribbled on her pad, tore the order off in one quick jerk and clipped it over the griddle. The fat man touched it with his thick fingers and dropped another patty. The meat hissed and popped. In a few minutes he flipped the patty and slapped on two pieces of American cheese. There were fries already going in a basket in the deep fryer and he shook the basket every minute or so.

The waitress brought my beer and water. Before she could get away, I asked her where the town cemetery was.

"Which one?"

"Saints Rest."

"That's out north of town, I believe. Hey, Mike," she said over her shoulder. "Where's that Saints Rest Cemetery? Is that on 231 or 15?"

"15," Mike said.

"Take 15 North," she said. "It's about five miles past the junction."

I watched Mike plate my food, then he rang a bell and shouted, "Order up!" even though the waitress was standing right in front of him. There were three other people seated at the counter and a few more had come in and sat in booths and Mike was beginning to work at a faster pace to keep up. The waitress brought my food and gave me a bottle of ketchup and two napkins.

"You going to a funeral?" she asked, looking at what I was wearing—an old Corona T-shirt, jeans, and jogging shoes.

"Just visiting a grave. A cousin of mine. His name was DeeRay Landwehr. He lived here for a while and died sometime back. Did you know him?"

She thought for a minute. "I don't know any DeeRays. Hey, Mike, you know anybody named DeeRay who died?"

"What's that?" Mike said. He had to shout over the sound of fries going hard in the fryer.

"You know any DeeRays?"

"I don't know any DeeRays. I know some Dicks, though," and he laughed at himself. "Who's asking?"

"This man here. The graveyard man."

"Who you looking for?"

"I'm not really looking for anyone, just a cemetery."

Mike grunted then went back to his grill.

"Do you know anybody named Vanessa?" I asked.

The waitress scrunched her face and thought. "Don't ring a bell," she said finally. "Why, did she die, too?"

"No," I said. "She's alive and kicking. So maybe you can tell me where this is?" I pulled Vanessa's address from my pocket and showed it to her.

"That's out on Breckinridge Road, past the stockyards. Just head west until you smell the cows."

I finished my burger and fries, drank the water and nursed the beer. The waitress was busy with customers and Mike was working like a mad organist at the griddle. I left a twenty and some change on the counter and walked out.

The sun was high and warm and the town was bustling with lunchtime traffic. I got in my car and headed down Main and left the center of town and the buildings behind, as if Garrison, like many small towns, suddenly dried up or couldn't grow past an invisible barrier and turned into empty lots, then trees. I found State Highway 15, a narrow two-lane lined with tall pines, and traveled north for about five miles before I saw a sign that read "Cemetery," with an arrow pointing to a dirt road. I made the turn and the trees thickened into a solid dark wall and the dust flew from my tires and built a piling red cloud behind me. I slowed and turned under an iron arch that read *Saints Rest*, like a sign over the entrance to a cattle ranch. I followed a narrow, barely visible path into the cemetery. There was a bluish cinderblock building in the center of the grounds, and a yellow, hulking backhoe parked near one wall. The gravestones were lined in neat rows, though some of the older ones leaned like they were sinking into quicksand. The road horseshoed around the outer reaches of the cemetery, skirted by woods, and I stopped at the top of the bend and got out.

Nan had emailed me a hand drawn map of the cemetery so I could find the grave. It was drawn like a pirate's treasure map, showing the curved road, the small building represented by a simple square, with dashes indicating steps I should take, and an "X" marking the location of the grave. Soon, I was standing over the grave of my dead cousin. The marker read "DeeRay Willis Landwehr," and then the years of his life. That was it. No engraved angels, no bible verses, no fancy catch phrases.

I bowed a little, then put my hands together like I was going to say a prayer, which is something I never did, so my mind went blank. All I could think to say, finally, was, "It's good to see you again," and "Rest in peace," which seemed silly as soon as I said the words out loud. I placed a small memorial wreath of blue and red plastic flowers I bought at Walmart back home on Cousin DeeRay's grave, stood there for another thirty seconds or so, then walked back in my car.

The sky was clear and bright and I felt good about what I had done.

Before I left home, my wife said I should stay out of it. "Why are you so interested in her? Don't bother the poor woman," she said.

"But she knows things," I said. "When I spoke with her on the phone, it sounded like she wanted to talk to me."

"Why would she do that? Unless she's after something."

"I don't think she has any family now."

"Did she say that?"

"It was her silence that spoke volumes," I said.

When I reached the outskirts of Garrison, I headed east, like the waitress had said to do, and looked for the stockyards, then Breckinridge Road. I was only a few miles off the highway when I smelled the cattle and saw up ahead what looked like miles of feedlots crowded with dark moving shapes, all destined for the slaughterhouse. I couldn't hold my breath long enough to get beyond the rancid smell so I breathed through my mouth until my throat turned dry. Before long, I hit a crossroad and made a right. The drainage ditches were tall with weeds and the one railroad track I crossed looked to be an abandoned line. The road itself crumbled at the edge like a ragged fault line and the pines crept closer and closer, threatening to encircle my car.

I came upon a couple of trailer houses, both tucked inside a dark cave of pine, and only the mailbox numbers distinguished them. I had written down Box 125 on the piece of paper I carried in my shirt pocket. When 125 appeared on a mailbox I turned into a sandy drive that wound through the trees and ended at a yellow trailer with a rust-pocked white pick-up out front. There was a metal swing set on a bare dirt patch and a pair of bicycles upended like skeletons in the front yard, and a small plastic swimming pool overturned near the bikes. A cat, gray as a rain cloud, came out from under the skirting, stretched, then jumped on the hood of my car. I got out and scratched it behind its ears. It was an old cat with green eyes and battle scars on its face and back.

I walked up the three metal steps to the door and knocked. A woman opened the door and poked her head out. Her hair was blonde and short and spiked all over, her eyes dark. She was petite and I looked down to talk to her.

"Vanessa?" I asked.

"Who wants to know?" she said, wiped her chin with the collar of her black T-shirt.

"I'm Bill Landwehr, from Oklahoma." Her eyes showed no sign of recognition. "DeeRay's cousin," I said. "We spoke on the phone?"

"That guy that called in the middle of the night?"

"Yes," I said, slightly embarrassed. "I came down to lay a wreath at DeeRay's grave and thought I would like to meet you."

She looked beyond me to my car, and at the cat leaving paw prints on the windshield. "You came all that way for *what?*"

"To meet you," I said. "Maybe to talk about DeeRay."

She made a sound like *humph*, looked again at my car, back at me, then, to my surprise, opened the door wide and motioned me inside.

I had never been inside a trailer house before and it felt like I stepped into a freight car with furniture—a little claustrophobic, dimly lit by a single lamp and natural light through the small curtains. There was a small tan sofa and a blue recliner, a round coffee table in the middle, and pictures on the walls of children and adults, photographed singly and in pairs. In the corner was a cardboard box that bulged with the chaos of toys.

"Would you want something to drink?" Vanessa asked. In addition to the dark T-shirt, she wore black cut-off jeans and red-striped socks. Her face was thin, her lips narrow and pink, and with her short, spiked hair, her ears stuck out like a child's after a haircut.

"I could do with something."

"You want Coke or sweet tea or something else?"

"Anything is fine," I said.

"I'm having a Coke."

"I'll have one as well, then."

"I don't have any ice," she said, "but it's cold from the fridge."

"I don't need ice," I said, and then she came from the kitchen with two cans of Coke and offered me one without opening it.

"Pop a top," she said, "and have a seat."

I opened the soda and took a short drink, then sat on the couch. It gave way as if it had no springs and I sat with my knees higher than my hips. Vanessa sat on the edge of the recliner. After a moment of awkward silence, I said, "So how long have you lived here?"

"Long while," she said. "Me and DeeRay bought the place, but the credit was mine and it was always in my name. It still is. I'm thinking of selling out, though, and taking an apartment in town. It'd be cheaper that way in the long run, I think. I work at the Short-Stop over by the ballpark. When Charlie makes me Assistant Manager, I figure me and the kids will make the move."

"How many kids do you have?" I asked.

"Three in all," she answered flatly, like she was counting coasters on the coffee table. "Only one belongs to DeeRay, though, my youngest boy. The other boy, the oldest, came from a fellow I met in Beaumont, but we didn't really hit it off for long. He's almost twelve. DeeRay Jr. is eight and a half. And there's a little baby who ain't here right now. She's with my mama in town."

I took a sip of soda, then said, "I'd like to meet your kids."

Vanessa eyed me without saying a word, and then startled me when she suddenly shouted, "Boys!"

"What!" came the answer from a room down the narrow hallway.

"Don't 'what' me you two. Get in here and meet somebody."

I heard shuffling feet, a door open, then a boy wearing the gangly body of a teenager appeared. He had his mother's eyes and hair color.

"This is Rowdy, my first and oldest. This is your stepdaddy's cousin."

"Bill," I said, and reached out and shook his limp hand. "Good to meet you, Rowdy," I said, to which the boy only nodded.

"Mama?" he said. "Ain't there something to eat in the kitchen?"

"If you hunt up something for yourself, there is," Vanessa said.

"Well, if I have to get it myself . . ." he started to say, and went back to where he had come from.

Then a second boy arrived. I was stunned by his appearance. It was if I was looking at a moment frozen in time, some leftover image unaffected by memory for decades. Cousin DeeRay stood before me just as I remembered him, broad in the shoulders, thick chest, with large, round limbs. Even his hair was combed in the same way, a wave of dark locks pushed back over the top of his head.

"This is DeeRay, Jr. Most people just call him DeeRay, though, because he don't like to be called Junior. DeeRay, this is your daddy's cousin, Billy, from Oklahoma."

"Bill Landwehr," I said, and shook his hand. His grip was strong for a kid. "Me and your dad were great friends when we were young, and if you don't mind my saying, you are the spitting image of him."

DeeRay Jr. looked at his mother, then back at me. "That's what everybody says," he muttered with some disappointment.

"I mean, it makes me feel like I'm twelve again and ready to climb trees with your dad."

"I'm just eight, almost nine," DeeRay Jr. said. "But when I'm twelve, I'll have a BB gun. Right Mama?"

"That depends," Vanessa said, then, "Now sit down and talk to your daddy's cousin while I make some turkey sandwiches. If you got time to stay a minute?" she said, looking at me.

"Sure. I've got nothing but time."

While Vanessa rummaged around the kitchen, DeeRay Jr. stared at me and I stared at him.

"What grade you in?"

"Going on third," he said.

"That's a good grade."

"I suppose," he said, then started chewing on his fingernails. "I remember my daddy," he said.

"Your dad and me, we practically grew up together. Do you play football?"

"Nope."

"Your dad was a fine player. Big and strong."

"I remember him," he said, as if he were trying to convince himself it was true. "What do you do?"

"I teach."

"Are you rich?" he asked.

"Not at all."

He blinked hard a couple of times, as if trying to get me into focus. "You got any kids my age?"

"No," I said. "Just cats."

"How many cats you got?"

"Two."

"We got just one, but that's enough. How many dogs you got?"

"None," I said.

"We got two but you might not ever see them."

His mother asked from the kitchen if I wanted mayo or mustard on my sandwich. "Mustard is great," I said, then, to DeeRay Jr., "Do you like school?"

"No sir," he said. "My teacher is an old hag and she don't like me very much so I spend a lot of time in the hall."

"What do you do that gets you sent to the hall?"

"Just trouble in general. I hit kids sometimes, but not every time they need it. They say things, so I pop them in the chops. Not so hard as I can, though."

"What do they say?"

"Well," he said, "sometimes they say I'm poorer than Aunt Gerty's goat. Sometimes they call me fatty. So I get after them. That's what Jubal says to do."

"Who's Jubal?"

"My baby sister's daddy. He lives in Nacogdoches and comes to visit once a week to hold her and give her toys."

Vanessa came in carrying three paper plates, one in the crook of her elbow, and one in each hand. She gave me a sandwich and some chips. "Go tell that brother of yours I have sandwiches."

"Why don't you go tell him yourself?" DeeRay said roughly.

"Such backtalk," Vanessa said, glancing at me, then she shouted, "Rowdy! Eats are here!"

Rowdy came out of his room.

"I set you a place at the table," she said.

"What is it?"

"Turkey and chips, and I gave you the last pickle from the jar."

Rowdy looked at me for a second, then went into the kitchen and sat at the table. We ate our sandwiches and drank our Cokes.

"How long you in town for?" Vanessa asked, her mouth full of bread and meat.

I finished chewing, said, "Just today. I'll head back toward home this afternoon."

She nodded, chewed, and made a sound like she was humming to herself.

"That's a nice car you got there. Looks brand new. It must have set you back some."

"All of them set you back some," I said.

She chewed. DeeRay Jr. chewed. "You know," Vanessa finally said, "Your cousin was a decent man, but he couldn't hold on to money. He bought too much you-know-what to keep food on the table most of the time, and when he passed, I ended up paying for all his mistakes. DeeRay Jr. grinds his teeth something terrible, but it costs three hundred dollars to get a special mouth guard made so he'll stop it."

DeeRay Jr. said, "I do it like this," and he ground his teeth together to show me. "Sometimes I get a headache in the night from it."

"I'm sorry to hear that," I said. "I'm a snorer myself. I even went to a sleep clinic once. I have to sleep on my side."

Vanessa made the sound like humming again, then said, "DeeRay, you and Rowdy go on out and play."

"I'm still eatin'," Rowdy protested from the kitchen.

"Take your brother outside like I said," and Rowdy shoved the kitchen chair back roughly and then went to hold the door open for DeeRay Jr.

"Can we at least sit in your car, Mister?" Rowdy asked.

My first inclination was to say no, but I checked my pocket to make sure I had the keys and told him it was all right with me.

"Don't touch anything but the door handle and your asses on the seats," Vanessa said.

"We won't," DeeRay Jr. said.

After the door shut behind them, Vanessa was quiet. She took the time to finish her sandwich. "Those boys are good boys," she said, finally. "Rowdy is a hard worker and does well by his little brother and baby sister. DeeRay Jr.'s a good boy, too, only he's mad a lot of the time because his daddy died and didn't leave him much of anything. My mama helps some, but it's awful hard to raise three on what I make. The worst part is that DeeRay's family isn't any help at all. That Nan won't even speak to me anymore, even though I'm raising her own nephew." She paused to let her complaint hang in the air, then asked, "I don't suppose you could spare some money, could you? I mean, you are pretty much family and I wouldn't ask otherwise. It just seems you are a caring man to come all this way to see us all in DeeRay's name."

"Sure," I said. "How much do you need?"

"Would a couple of hundred be going too far?"

"In my current circumstances, yes," I said, knowing I only had about a hundred bucks in my wallet, and I suddenly didn't feel very generous. Still, I opened my wallet and gave Vanessa fifty dollars. "That's all I have to spare, I'm afraid. I wish I had more to give you."

"I appreciate it," she said, nodding, then lit a cigarette and leaned back in the recliner. She looked at me, drawing on her cigarette until the ashes hung long. "You don't look much like DeeRay. To be family, I mean."

"No, we don't look anything alike. But his dad and my dad were brothers, and they didn't look much alike either."

She crushed out her cigarette. "I suppose that makes sense then," she said, took a sip of Coke from the can resting in the cupholder in the chair arm. "DeeRay's dad was a child molester. I suppose you knew that already."

"Yes," I said. "I've heard the story."

"What about your dad?"

"He was not a molester," I said. "He was an accountant." Then I told her about my dad working for a small accounting firm for almost thirty-five years and my mother being a librarian, and that both had passed a few years back. "In fact, they died three days apart," I added, just because it made them sound devoted to each other, even though my parents could barely stand to be in the same room together for most of their marriage.

"I've heard of such things happening. Sounds really sweet," she said. "You got any brothers or sisters?" I said no, and took another drink of Coke. "Kids?"

"No children," I said, then added, as if I needed to explain, "It just didn't happen for us."

She looked a little surprised. "I thought I heard you say you were a teacher."

"Yes. That's right."

"What grade?"

"Actually, I teach at the college level."

"That makes sense, I guess. Grown-ups are easier. History?"

"English," I said.

She pinched at her spikes of hair, said, "That's interesting."

"Not really."

"What about your wife? She work?"

"Insurance. She works at an insurance office."

"What's her name?"

"Candace," I said.

"Does she go by Candy?"

"No. She hates when people call her Candy."

"Too bad," she said. "I think Candy is a nice name. Some people call me Nessie. Like that sea monster," and she smiled and laugh, then coughed a little. "You know," she said after clearing her throat, "I went to college for a whole semester. I wanted to be a nurse's assistant. But then Rowdy came, and then came the breakup with his daddy, then DeeRay, of course, and DeeRay Jr., then all the shit that happened afterwards. And now the baby."

"What's her name?" I asked.

"Sandra, after my mama. But we don't call her Sandy. We got to calling her Bingo because that's what my mama said after she found out it was a girl and not another boy. *Bingo!* she says. And it stuck."

"That's a good name for a kid, I suppose. What's that old song? About the farmer's dog?"

Vanessa looked at me. "I know it. Use to sing that in primary school. But that's not the same kind of Bingo we mean," she said. She dug her finger around the cigarette pack for the last one, wadded up the package, and then pinched the cigarette between her lips. Then she took it out without lighting it. "Why did you come all the way down here after I hung up on you? You seem to be a smart man. Even a pretty nice man from what I can tell. But I've known some thick-headed mean people as well. Those I don't usually let into my house and feed them lunch." She smiled, lit the cigarette, took a deep draw, and blew smoke at the ceiling.

"Like I said, I just wanted to visit my cousin's grave, and talk to his wife." We sat quietly until I felt we had reached the end of it, so I stood up, said, "I thank you for your time, and the sandwich and Coke. It hit the spot."

She smiled at me. I expected her to tell me to sit back down, and I felt bad about standing up in the first place. "It all kind of adds up in a funny way if you think about it," she said.

"What's that?"

"Well," she said, "if it weren't for me and DeeRay having DeeRay Jr, you'd be the very last of your family line. Not counting your wife, of course."

"That's not quite true," I said. "There's Nan. And she has kids. In fact, we plan to meet up in Kansas before Christmas."

Vanessa shook her head. "She's not really one of you. She'd be like a half cousin, maybe? I'm not even sure there is such a thing. DeeRay was your cousin cousin, and DeeRay Jr. is your second cousin. See how that all works itself out?"

"Sure," I said, already fishing in my pocket for my car keys.

She took a long drag from her cigarette, this time exhaling the smoke in my direction. "You want to know why I hung up on you that night?"

"I could hazard a few guesses. I was a little drunk, if I remember correctly, you didn't know me, and it was late. Is that about right?"

She waved away my explanation, as if those were common occurrences in her life. She stood up and moved closer to me. For a second, I thought she was going to put her cigarette out on my chest, but instead she took my hand in hers and held it. I felt the money I had given her pressed into my palm.

"Never mind about this," she said, then, "It's been nice to meet you, Cousin Bill. Maybe me and the kids can come visit you and Candy when school's out? You know I've never been to Oklahoma? And it's just right there," she said, pointing to the ceiling. "I've never been much of anywhere. It seems like I'm stuck in Garrison, waiting it all out."

I didn't ask her what it was she was waiting out. Maybe the hope she was being promoted to assistant manager at the Short-Stop. Maybe everything Cousin DeeRay had left behind for her to sort on her own. I was already thinking about the drive home, the need for gas, some coffee to keep me awake. I decided I would call my wife, tell her I was still in Garrison, but on my way home, and that I wasn't going to stop for the night. She would tell me not to push it, to get a hotel room if I needed to. But if I did try it all in one go, I should call her every hour or so, or if I felt myself dozing off. That way she would know I was all right.

Then the front door flew open so hard it banged against the side of the recliner. DeeRay Jr. leaned in and shouted, "Mama, the damn cat got in the car!"

"Get it out, then," she calmly said.

"I can't reach it. It's under the front seat and I can't get hold of it. I've tried already *five times*."

"Tell Rowdy to get it, then. His arms are longer."

"I can't, Mama. He's already gone down the road. He said it was my fault the cat got in and he won't help get it out." He was sweating, his voice cracking like he was about to cry. His hands were pressed firmly against both sides of the narrow door jamb, arms locked at the elbows, as if he were trying to split the trailer in half. I took a step toward the door, but I knew there was no way around him to get to my car and remove the cat. No one was going in or out with him standing in the doorway like that.

There was Cousin DeeRay again, waiting for me to make a run at him down Mims Road with a football tucked nervously against my chest. I knew what I was looking at.

Natural Horsemanship

Sandy and Mark Downing lived on ten acres just off County Rd 48. They operated a miniature horse farm they called Tiny Equine Breeding. So far, they owned only one pony but were looking to add one more by fall. The following year they hoped to have a foal to sell.

They sat together on the couch on Sunday night and ate tacos. Each had a standing dinner tray. Mark made his famous guacamole dip, and Sandy stirred up a pitcher of margaritas. They crunched tacos and dipped tortilla chips and sipped their drinks while they watched a man on TV start a young, unbroken horse. He made the horse circle the round pen by holding a long flexible pole with a plastic bag attached to the end. The noise from the bag spooked the horse, so the horse moved away from it. After a few turns around the pen, the trainer made the horse stop and go the other direction. Sometimes the horse only trotted, at others broke into a long, anxious lope. By the time the session was over, if all worked out, the trainer would put a blanket and saddle on the horse and lead him out of the round pen.

"It's just groundwork, but he's building up trust," Mark said. "He's using a natural method."

Sandy said, "Natural horsemanship."

Mark said, "That's it. Just look how relaxed that gelding is. Beautiful."

"Smidge needs some groundwork like that," Sandy said. "She's so nervous she won't stand for the farrier."

"Smidge is a wonderful pony," Mark said, "and she'll be a beautiful mother one day." He took a big bite out of a taco. Some of the filling fell out and landed on his tray. He pinched the scattered pieces of meat and lettuce and cheese and dropped them into his mouth.

The horse trainer wore a headset with a flesh-colored microphone. He talked about how important it was to truly connect to the animal. "When the horse really locks onto you," he said, "you've got him." Then he demonstrated by walking slowly away. The horse was standing at the back of the round pen, breathing heavily, but when the trainer walked off, the horse pricked its ears and took a few steps toward the trainer. Pretty soon the horse was following the trainer around the pen. The audience of onlookers, sitting on metal bleachers, clapped at the sight.

"He's locked on," Mark said. "Do you see that, Sand? There's a real connection there."

Sandy had the margarita pitcher on the lamp table. There were thin, round slices of fresh lime pressed like green faces against the glass, and some floating just under the ice cubes. She poured herself another, then held up the pitcher.

"No thanks," Mark said. "I'll wait a bit. I'm swimming already."

The horse trainer had the blanket on the horse in no time, and then another man, who hadn't been on screen before, stepped through the gate and into the round pen carrying a saddle.

Sandy said, "I'm not sure it's going to work."

Mark said, "What do you mean? That's a real horse trainer."

Sandy shifted on the couch and bumped the tray with her knee and nearly tipped it over. "I mean I don't think he'll get the saddle on him."

"Sure he will," Mark said. "Besides, they wouldn't show it if he didn't, would they? They wouldn't broadcast a flop. They'd just edit it out and try again."

"I don't know," she said. "That colt looks like he's scared to me. Maybe it's the person holding the saddle. Maybe he just doesn't like *him.*"

"He's fine. He's locked on," Mark insisted.

The trainer walked over, took the saddle, and the other man left the pen and closed the gate. The trainer hung the stirrups on the saddle horn, placed the saddle on the horse's back, then gently let down one stirrup, walked around the horse, and let down the other.

"See there?" Mark said. "That man is a natural."

"But the other man left," Sandy said. "The one that brought the saddle. That's the one I think the horse was scared of. If *he'd* tried to drop that saddle, things would be different."

"Sure," Mark said. "But he was just the helper, wasn't he? He hadn't made a real connection. As far as the horse was concerned, he didn't even exist."

Sandy scooped some guacamole with a chip, chewed slowly, finally said, "I suppose you're right." She took another chip, scooped a blob of dip, and held it out to him.

"I'll take it," Mark said. "I can't get enough of the stuff."

On a Friday afternoon the doorbell rang. Sandy was home, but Mark was in town buying a new faucet for the bathroom sink. She was in the bedroom with a window that looked out onto the porch, so she parted the curtains. There was a man wearing a green muscle shirt and camouflage cargo shorts that hung crooked at his waist. He had a large dog on a rope leash.

She walked down the hall and slowly opened the front door but kept the screen door closed and locked. Before she could say anything, the man smiled. He was missing one of his front teeth. He was sweating through his muscle shirt.

"How are you this morning?" he said.

"Can I help you?" Sandy asked. She put her hand on the door handle.

"Ma'am, are you by chance missing a dog?" He pointed at the dog. The dog stretched the rope leash tight and was near the edge of the porch. The man tried to pull it closer, but the dog didn't give.

Sandy looked at the dog. "That's not ours. We don't own a dog."

"That's too bad," he said. "She's a really nice one. I was just wondering if you ever seen her before? You have a very nice set-up here, by the way. I saw your sign about miniature horses. I love horses. How many you got on hand?"

"Just the one," Sandy said. "We just started."

The man scratched his chin with his middle finger. He was missing part of his index finger down to the knuckle. "I guess you always start with one, right? Did I say horses are just about my favorite animal? Anyway, I was just passing by, and I saw this dog on the road, and thought I'd try to find her rightful owner."

Sandy said, "Not us. Sorry." She stepped back to close the door, but the man held up his hand that was missing part of a finger.

"Excuse me, Ma'am, but do you think you could keep her for a bit, then? Just a short while? At least until I can find a place for her. Would you consider that? It won't take me long. You can see she's a really nice dog. Skinny, but nice." He pulled at the leash again but the dog held her ground. Her tongue was hanging out and dripped.

Sandy said, "I'm sure she is a nice dog. But we couldn't take her."

The man wiped sweat from his forehead with the back of his hand. "I'm sad to hear that. It would be a shame if she got runned over." He tugged on the leash again. "Could I ask you for one thing then, Ma'am? Could you maybe point me to a water hose? Me and the dog could use a drink."

Sandy pointed. "Round back by the horse trough there's a spigot and hose. Help yourself, just make sure you shut it off."

"I will," he said. "I'll make double sure. But you wouldn't happen to have a bowl I might use for the dog? Maybe an old margarine bowl?"

"I don't have any margarine bowls," she said. "Just real ones."

"That's fine," he said. "I just remember when people used to keep that sort of thing around. I ate Lucky Charms out of margarine bowls every morning when I was a kid." He scratched his chin again. "I guess that don't happen much anymore."

"I couldn't say either way," Sandy said, then she closed the door and locked it.

She walked to the bedroom, turned on the TV, and waited. There was a soap opera on. A couple sat in a restaurant and talked about how sorry they both were their marriage hadn't lasted. The music was slow and sad, then it cut to a detergent commercial. Sandy got up from the edge of the bed and peeked through the curtains. The porch was empty.

After the soap ended, she put on her muck boots and went outside to water the pony. The dog was tied to a fence post by the water spigot. She peeked inside the barn and saw the man in the stall petting Smidge. He looked at her.

"You ought not be in here," she said, taking a step back. "That pony don't like people she don't know."

The man pulled at his cargo shorts that sagged on one side, then ran his fingers over the pony's blond mane, then along her withers and back. "She maybe five years old?" he asked. Smidge stomped a front leg to shed a few flies. The flies disappeared, then quickly returned to the same leg.

"My husband is just about home," Sandy said. "He won't like you being back here."

The man looked along the barn's warped shelves until he spotted a bottle of fly repellent. He took the bottle, adjusted the nozzle, then walked around the pony and misted each leg down to the hoof, then along her back and rump. "They're bad this time of year," he said. "Ever tried a fly mask on her?"

Sandy took the fly spray bottle from him and put it back on the shelf. "She doesn't like wearing it. She'll rub it off every time."

"Head shy is she?" He stood by the pony's shoulder, slowly moved his hand up to the withers, then the poll, and down her forehead. The pony pitched her head when he reached the muzzle. "Will she take a halter?"

"Yes."

"Flat nylon or rope?"

"Flat nylon."

The man touched the muzzle again and the pony lifted her head. "She's a little sore there. I'd go with a natural rope halter if I were you. Easier on the skin." He shooed a fly from his own cheek, walked around the horse, stopped at her rump, then leaned over and gently slid his hand down to the fetlock. He clicked his tongue and the pony lifted her hoof. He pressed his thumb into the sole, ran his finger around the hoof wall. He released the leg, then went around to check the other three, clicking his tongue, pressing the sole, circling the hoof wall with his finger.

"She stands well," he said. "Must be easy on the farrier."

Sandy shook her head.

"No?" the man said, patting the pony on the back. "That's odd. She's still as a post for me. I'd ask your guy to leave a little more hoof on the next trim, though. He's cutting a tad short, in my opinion."

"I'll be sure to tell my husband when he gets home in a minute. He just went to get a faucet so he's coming right back."

The man patted the rump of the pony again. "I get it," he said, then, "Yep, you got a good solid pony here. She'll make some nice foals for you if you find the right stud to cover her."

Sandy pulled at her shirt collar.

The man cleared his throat. "I hate to repeat myself," he said, "but I wonder if I might leave that dog with you after all? I'm parked right down the road. I just don't have a place to keep her, you know? To be honest, I'm living in my car at the moment. Everything I own is in it. Stuffed to the gills. I'm ashamed to say it, but that's my current situation. If I had a place, I'd hang on to her. She's a fine dog. You can see that for yourself. I'm just hoping you might reconsider taking her in for a bit? You strike me as a kind person. Am I right? I can usually tell if I'm talking to a kind person."

Sandy said, "We try to be, me and my husband both."

"Sure you do," he said. "So if you can find it in your heart to take this dog, and maybe spare a few dollars, I'd very much appreciate you *and* your husband. I'm pretty much out of gas and, shamed as I am to say it, I've missed a few meals lately. If I can solve these few little problems with your help, I'd be grateful. Would that be possible?" He slipped one hand into the large side pocket of his cargo shorts and looked at her. "Does that sound like a deal you could live with?"

When he pulled a gun out of his pocket and pointed it at her, Sandy covered her face. She rocked back and forth and groaned.

"What good will it do you?" he said, taking a step toward her. "Better to just stand still and not think too much about it." Sandy stopped rocking, slowly slid her hands down her face. "Don't make me nervous, now. And there's no reason to make a show of it. I know your husband will be home soon."

"I lied," she said. "He's not coming back very soon at all."

The man rubbed sweat from his eyes and blinked hard. "Well, then, I suppose it won't hurt for me to sit and wait for a bit after all, will it? I can go in your house and pick up anything I might need after we're done here. Maybe rest up a little. Then I'll meet with your husband when he finally makes it home from wherever he might be at the moment."

"Just please let me show you where everything is. I've got some necklaces and rings," she begged. "There's some cash, too. You're welcome to it. Just follow me right into the house and I'll show you." The man was already shaking his head, but she kept talking. "Look, I'll make it real easy on you," she said. She took a sudden deep breath as if something had finally dislodged from her throat. The man tightened his grip on the gun. "Listen to me. I'll take that dog after all. Let me do that for you, and along with it give you some food to carry back to your car. We could use a good dog around here. I'll take her off your hands and take good care of her, too."

The man laughed quietly to himself. "I don't think you understand the situation."

"Sure I do," Sandy said. She swiped at the strands of hair stuck to her cheek. "I know exactly the situation. But just look how behaved that pony is for you. She don't behave for me at all, I can tell you. Or the farrier. Or the vet when she comes around, either." Sandy swallowed hard. "Or my husband for that matter. Truth is, that pony can't stand him, and barely tolerates me." She crossed her arms. "You know as well as I do we don't know what the hell what we're doing out here. Right? We'll never make a nickel on horses."

"That, lady, comes as no real surprise to me, as you might imagine."

"But you," she said, "you're a natural. I can see that."

The man laughed, leaned back on his heels. "All I did was muck out stalls for ten bucks a day at a racetrack. But that's where I learned just enough to not get kicked in the head while doing it. That's my primary knowledge when it comes to horses, but it's got real-life applications, if you get me."

Sandy nodded her head. The pony shifted her stance. Then, with her arms still crossed, Sandy took a small, shuffled step toward him.

"I wouldn't," he said flatly.

The next sound Sandy made was a broken, nervous hiss that barely moved past her teeth. The next was richer, followed by another. "Shush," she said. "Just shush a minute."

"What's this about?" the man said.

"Take it easy," she said quietly, then raised her hand and reached toward him.

The man took a step back. "Scoot right against that wall there now. Right by that pony. Don't do anything else," he said, waving the gun at her. "And lady, let me tell you this while I've got your full attention: I wouldn't leave that dog out there with you if you paid me."

Sandy stood motionless. The pony shifted in the stall. Dust floated in the shaft of light that spilled from the one high window above the wooden beams. "You made a connection with that dog, didn't you?" she said finally. "I know it for sure. I can see it. You won't even need that rope leash anymore. You won't have to tug her along like you've been doing. She'll just follow you wherever you go."

"Of course she will," he said. "You've got that much right at least. And she's not even mine. Let's just say I borrowed her from some folks a day or so ago. And trust me, they won't miss her a bit." Sandy took a step back. "Don't try running away," he said.

"I'm not about to," she said. "But let's at least bring that poor dog in here where it's cool, why don't we? Let's not let her stand out there tied by a spigot she can't even get a drink from. You can follow me out there and watch the whole time while I untie her, and we'll come right back in here."

The man squinted. "Just hold up a minute," he said, and he wiped at his eye with the back of his hand that held the gun. "You should've just given me bowl like I asked for. She wouldn't be standing out there so thirsty if she could've had a nice bowl to lap from."

Sandy nodded, then turned toward the barn entrance. "I should've," she said.

"And me a cup. It's not right that a grown man should have to suck at a hose."

"I should've," Sandy said, and she walked slowly out into the sunlight with the man following close behind.

"And let *me* get that knot she's tied with," he said. "It's not what you think it is. If you pull the wrong way, it won't budge. That's because it holds the horse, or whatever you got attached to it, tight as a tick, but pull the long tail of it, it comes off easy." The man patted the dog on the head before he gave the end of the rope a jerk and the rope dropped from the post. "See there?"

Sandy nodded. "It's called a quick-release knot. Safer for horse and human. Every responsible horse owner should know it, but I doubt you do."

"I don't," Sandy said, and turned to walk back toward the barn.

He looked down at the dog, whose head drooped in the heat. "You hear that, girl? She's never even heard of such a knot," and he followed Sandy inside.

Mark came home with the new faucet and spent over an hour taking the old one off and setting and caulking the new one on the sink and attaching the new water lines. When he finished, he gathered his tools and the old copper lines that had greened over the years, then went into the living room, then tried the kitchen, then the utility room. In each room he said, "Sand?"

He neatly arranged the tools in the toolbox, closed the lid and set the latch, then carried the heavy toolbox to the barn where he stored it.

When the gun went off the pony ran headfirst into the barn wall before she gathered herself, turned, and sped out the open stall, then through the pasture gate with its chain hanging loose from the post. Mark was on the back steps when the pony ran past him. She went around the side of the house, slipped on the grass, raced past the car parked in the driveway, and out to the dirt road. By the time she reached the crossroads at the top of the hill she had slowed to a trot.

At the trailer house, just over the hill, Linzie Carmichael pedaled her bicycle in a circle around an old tractor that died in the yard five years earlier. Her daddy hadn't been able to get it running again and left it where it quit. For Linzie it was the summer between second and third grade, and she no longer needed training wheels on her bike. On her fifth time around the tractor, she heard a loud pop in the distance, and on the fourteen time around, a pony appeared at her mailbox. She dropped her feet to stop her bike and saw the pony with its head held high, neck arched, ears erect, shoulders darkened by sweat. Linzie slowly tipped her bike to the ground. She took a few steps, but the pony suddenly wheeled back toward the road. Linzie walked to the end of her dirt driveway and watched until the pony stopped to feed on the grass at the road's edge, her long blond tail nervously sweeping the air.

Mark stepped inside the barn and dropped the toolbox. It clattered loudly against the floor and the latch sprung open and tools skittered away.

The man squatted in the corner of Smidge's stall, back against the barn clapboards. His arms hung loose at his sides, his head turned slightly away, chin resting hard against his chest. A dark wound glistened high on his cheek, and he was perfectly still.

Sandy stood in the opposite corner of the stall, the dog beside her. When Mark came in and dropped the toolbox and looked at her, she raised one hand and covered her mouth. Then she dropped the pistol she held in the other hand. It made a soft thud on the pine litter.

Mark stepped inside the stall and the dog growled and moved closer to Sandy. He tried to kick the dog away but missed, and just then the man's body started moving, although there was no life in it at all, and it fell out of the squat of its own accord and partly unfolded its legs until it settled in the pine shavings and didn't move again.

To Our Own Devices

Lily drew much comfort from her husband, Jack. Especially those first few weeks after Jimmy, their oldest, went to the state prison at Monroe for using a jagged beer bottle on a man's neck. But even family heartaches would not slow the plowing of a new road in faraway Center County, so he left her with the grandchildren for two months to ride a dozer through one-hundred-foot stands of Southern pine.

He was gone only a day when the grandchildren cornered a Tabby cat behind the rose bush outside her bedroom window. Lily stopped sweeping the pieces of wheat toast left from breakfast, pushed into a little brown pyramid on the blue-tiled floor, and listened to the cacophony of their voices.

"Bally-hooo! Bally-hooo!"

"Gimme something to chunk! Gimme me a pinecone! Gimme me a rock from the flowerpot, Jenny!"

"Get your own stupid rock."

"Shake the bush, why don't ya?"

"I need something to chunk."

"Don't make so much noise."

"Yoo-hoo, Kitty!"

"You're making him bristle."

"Here kitty kitty kitty kitty kitty."

Lily pushed the crumbs onto an old magazine and shook it clean over sink. She splashed the sides of the enameled basin, then stood with her fingertips slicing through the water flowing from the faucet. The cold steadied her nerves, relieved the tightness that gripped her forehead, settled her breathing. After a few long minutes, when she felt she might be able to stop breathing altogether without any ill effects, she turned off the water, dried her hands on a kitchen towel, and rolled the magazine so it fit neatly into the trash sack beneath the sink.

It was almost eleven, nearly time for lunch. The baloney needed slicing, lettuce washed, dill pickles fished out of the jar and quartered. The utensil drawer opened stubbornly, swollen by humidity. Her carving knife, a black-handled stainless Jack got her for Christmas, was buried under a potato masher, a silver whisk, a tangle of cookie cutters and a pair of beaters.

She put out the call for lunch at eleven-thirty.

"Bally-hooo!" Courtney sang, skipping into the kitchen.

Jenny already sat at the table with a black-haired doll, trying to feed it a corn chip. "Eat it, please," she said.

"Richey's afraid to leave," Courtney said, sliding next to her sister. "Afraid the cat might get away. Want me to get him, Granny?"

"Eat this one then," Jenny said to her doll, selecting a chip from a special pile she made next to her plate. She had a ring of red dirt around her chin and dribbles of grape Kool-Aid on her shirt.

Lily poured milk into three glasses. "Mind yourself," she told Courtney, who wrinkled her nose, pressed the tip of her pink tongue between her lips. Jenny paused to watch her sister and absent-mindedly ate a corn chip herself.

Lily went outside and around the house. Richey squatted on the ground, peering under the tangle of rose vines. "Leave it," Lily said. He looked up, rubbed his eyes with freckled, dirty fingers. He had her face, or at least her eyes, she thought, but his daddy, Jimmy's, square chin and hair color. Unlike the girls, with their brown hair and round faces, he had none of his mother's features. It was an absence Lily strangely regretted, despite her opinion of Darla, the abandoning mother, the weak wife. There was nothing soft about him, nothing needy or open or thin-skinned, and although he often teased his sisters to the point they pulled his hair or punched him in the stomach, he cried only a few spiteful tears. They couldn't muster the strength to make him shed more.

"I'm standing guard," he said, pulling at his belt loops. She stepped off the porch, stooped over his shoulder. "I think he's ready to bolt," he said. Beneath the windowsill, on bare, red ground, hunkered a large grey Tabby, feet drawn under, dull yellow eyes half-closed, tail curled around its legs like a striped snake. It let out a low growl.

"I don't think he's going to go anywhere. Looks like you scared him right into a nap."

Richey leaned over even further, his red hair dragging the ground. "I don't trust him."

"Come inside," Lily said.

"If I leave him, he'll take off."

"Maybe he won't."

"He's wild. Saw his tail puffed up when he went in."

"We'll watch for him later."

"I'm not hungry," he said, sitting down, crossing his legs.

"I didn't ask you if you were," Lily answered, feeling the grip tighten on her forehead. She grabbed his arm, tugged against his hard thin bone, and pulled him to her. She aimed at his ear with her mouth full of angry words, told him he had two seconds to get inside with his sisters. He drew his neck tight into his shoulders and tried to pull away from her. He groaned as if she was tearing his arm from the socket. It was enough to make Lily let go. Instead, she slid her hands under his arms and lifted. He was heavier than she thought. She only made his shoulders shrug.

"Hey!" he shouted, breaking into a laugh, "Those ain't handles!" He straightened, brushed the dirt from his knees, grinned belligerently.

"Move," she said, spinning him onto the porch, keeping her fingers pressed into his back, pushing him through the doorway.

He ran free of her, bellowing for help. He fell in beside his sisters, biting his nails, shaking his head, chattering his teeth, crying "I'm scared, Granny! Don't beat me, Granny!"

"Quiet!" Courtney yelled.

"Granny's gonna beat us all," Jenny said seriously to her doll, which made the other two laugh.

Lily ate standing next to the refrigerator, her back against the cool wall. They reminded her so much of her own four children, though her last boy was lost to leukemia. His death came slowly, marked by thinning cheeks. She measured his dying like she measured the growth of her first three, only his face with her fingers rather than standing him against the closet door and making a pencil mark. The other three did well, until Jimmy lost his temper in that bar. But her two girls were settled into good homes, with fairly good husbands. Neither daughter had children, but neither made any offers to take Jimmy's kids once the trouble started. Lily took them because she was experienced, and because she saw no alternative, though nearly sixty-seven, with thinning yellow hair, and a chronic shortness of breath.

Besides, with all the heartache and a certain coolness from her daughters after the trial, Lily felt the need to make some repairs, to keep the widening crack in the foundation of the family from swallowing everyone up. It was a flaw she believed existed from the very beginning; missing memories of her children when they were babies, toddlers, teenagers; memories, instead, of those headaches that came on sometimes, and the long naps she took that left blank spaces in her life. Those blank spaces, she worried, added up to a barroom brawl. Jack told her she had no apologies to make that didn't apply to him as well. But at least they had the grandchildren now, he said, and they were loved and well-tended to.

They all finished their sandwiches, Courtney by giving half to Richey, who stuffed the whole remaining portion into his mouth. Jenny left most of hers on the bench, mustard fingerprints all over it. Lily kept it on the counter for a while, thinking she might come back hungry after reassuring herself the cat was still there. By twelve-thirty they were standing at the rose bush again, Richey barking orders at his sisters, Jenny and Courtney refusing to do anything he demanded.

Lily wiped the tablecloth clean, then went into her bedroom. It was very warm. With the window open, she heard everything the children said. She took a pen from the top drawer of her bureau. The ink was nearly gone, pooled near the tip, but enough left for a letter to her husband, she thought. She also had five sheets of lemon-yellow stationery from the motel they stayed at during Jimmy's trial, along with some matching envelopes. She wrote the date at the top on the page—*July 18th, 1963. Dear Jack*, she wrote in tight little letters, then crossed out. Her hands dropped to her lap. It would not look good if she wrote too soon. He needed the distance, time on the dozer, time to get his hands sticky with pine tar, to wear out a pair of boot soles on the clutch and brake pedals, time to hear all the rumors circulate around the job site, whispers between his co-workers, questions about his son who made the newspapers. She crumpled up the piece of stationery, pulled another sheet onto her lap, and wrote, as neatly as her hand could manage, *Dear Jimmy*.

She didn't write more, but thought through all the things she might tell her son, especially that his children were fine, though Jenny was a little finicky about eating. Courtney gets louder and bossier by the day, and Richey, she recently discovered, has his father's chin. He is stubborn, like his father and grandad. He eats too fast, does everything too fast. Your dad is on a job in Center County, making a new road for whoever wants out or in. It will last two months. She misses him already, although it has only been a day. She has been left to her own devices. The weather is changing, getting hotter, more humid. The county social worker says everything looks good for the kids. Jack makes enough money. There is stability in the home. That's the word she likes to use. Stability. No one better suited for bringing up Courtney, Jennifer, and Richard. No one has heard from their mother, and no one really wants to. She is probably in New Mexico with her family. There she can stay. Her leaving the state makes everything easier, especially if it goes to a judge. They are in a home, with those most suited to raising them. Everything is going well, if only Jenny will eat more. *Dear Jimmy*, she wrote. *How are you? We are fine, though it is growing hotter.*

She put the letter aside. The ink pen rolled across the bed and clattered onto the floor before she could grab it. She caught brief glimpses through the rosebush of Jenny's doll, wrapped in her short, white arms, and Courtney's long brown hair, her once tidy braid unraveling across her back. Then she heard Richey tell Courtney to get his winter coat. "I'm gonna shield myself from the thorns."

"Granny'll beat you if you mess up those roses," Jenny said, laughing.

"I'm going *under* the roses, stupid."

"That sounds like a rotten idea," Courtney said.

Lily leaned over the wrought-iron bedstead, resting the undersides of her arms on the frame. She felt her damp skin suction to the top bar, arteries constricted by her own weight, hands already beginning to tingle. She lifted her eyebrows to break the grip on her forehead. She heard one of the children stomp across the porch, throw open the screen door, run to the hall closet. She heard the rattle of hangers, a door close, another open, feet on the porch, a fast walk outside through the dry grass. She knew it was Richey before he said, "Got it myself, you bums." He stood just outside the tangle of vines. She saw the blue coat rise in the air, then slip over his shoulders. "You go to that side," he demanded.

"I'm not doing any such thing."

"Me neither."

"I'll clobber both of you if you don't."

Courtney answered, deliberate and slow, "Oh-no-you-won't, Richard."

"Leave us alone," Jenny said.

"Do you want the cat or not?" he said finally, almost begging. The girls hesitated, then moved slowly around the bush, whispering to each other, Courtney telling Jenny they "would just stand there and that's all." He threatened to tell their daddy what sissies they were if they didn't cooperate. "I've got a dirt clod, so get ready."

"Kitty kitty kitty" Jenny called.

"Cover your eyes!" Richie shouted.

Courtney shouted, "Let it fly!"

Lily heard Richey take a deep breath, drawing energy from the heavy air that leaned against the house. He sucked in like slurping thick soup, held it in his mouth, then blew it out hard. The dirt clod thudded, broke apart, sent fragments rattling through the vines and leaves, ricocheted off the window screen. Before she saw it, she heard the cat spring suddenly against the window, bowing the screen outward, its claws curled through the now-enlarged holes, ears flat against its skull, yellow eyes wide in terror. Lily flinched, heard her sticky arms tear like tape from the bed frame as Richey twisted his fingers into the neck fur. She saw, in that final second of confusion, the cat's eyes slant sharply under the pressure to let go the screen.

And then, deep within her ears, further down than the children's voices could reach, she heard her pulse rising, like the sound of wind building in the treetops, growing, dying out, then gathering again. She attended to the sound as it came and went, and began to believe, with only an inkling of doubt, she could stay in that space, crouched and silent, until Jack came out of the pines, or Jimmy did his time, or until Darla stayed away just long enough to have to stay away forever.

And then Richey yelled "Gotcha!"

Lily opened her eyes, the heat in the room wrapped around her. She was surprised to find her hand pressed against her face, fingers splayed across her nose and mouth, the odor of baloney still strong on her palm.

"Pet him," Jenny said. "Let me pet him."

"Get away for a minute. I caught him."

After a pause, long enough to draw one full breath and let it out slowly, Lily got up from the bed and looked out the window through a break in the rose bush. They were moving away across the yard. She heard a low moan from the captured Tabby as Richey carried it to a shade tree near the road. The cat, all four feet spread into the air, twisting and squirming, was fast in his grip. He carried it far away from his body, deliberately swinging it in the direction of his sisters, making them run screaming with their faces covered.

Lily smoothed back her hair, parting it into damp rows with her fingers. She took up the letter she started to her son, then pulled the bed away from the wall and managed to scoot the pen out with her foot. She sat down, pressed the sheet of paper against her broad lap, erasing from her mind all the words of comfort she planned to write, knowing that he, of all people, could not believe her. *Dear Jimmy*, she read silently to herself. It was written in the neatest handwriting she could have managed. When she touched pen to paper again, she half-expected the ink to run dry before she ever got to what she really needed to say to him.

Catbirds

Great Grandpa Phillips, eyes closed, resting on his back, wearing round, gold-rimmed glasses, white cheeks ending in folds at the corners of his mouth like a bulldog's, lay in a casket in Grandma's living room. Grandma wore milky rubber gloves while she dressed him in his brown corduroy jacket and thin, black tie. She leaned over the casket like a mother over a bassinet. She was his only daughter, broad-nosed and stern.

My cousin Royce sat on the high bed in Grandma's bedroom. He was pale and excited. "Great-Grandpa Phillips is dead," he drawled, pronouncing *dead* as if saying it backwards. I sat in the big rocker in the corner and watched Royce flick his long, blonde hair out of his eyes. I had blonde hair then, too, but it was cut short and even across my forehead. We both had blue, German eyes, but my face was round from my mother's side of the family, his pointed at the chin, like my father's. And though we were both only ten years old, his body was already thickening while mine was determined to stay thin and angular.

Royce lived in a house with a tin roof and a wooden porch, built long before indoor plumbing made it to the pine thickets of East Texas. When Uncle Wayne finally decided to add a toilet, and later a bathtub, the kind that stood on white lion's feet, the flooring in Royce's bedroom was judged sturdiest. A yellow shower curtain hung from one wall to the next for privacy, but when the moon was full and shining through the tall window I stared hard at the dark, seated silhouette of my Aunt Paddy.

Royce owned a pellet gun and could identify every bird he picked off the high-line wires: mockingbirds, finches, English sparrows, red-winged blackbirds, starlings. He sent a catbird tumbling down to the ground just to show me the tiny whiskers growing from the sides of its beak. Afterwards, he unceremoniously tossed the still warm, gray body into the sunflowers and dusty black-eyed susans that grew thick beside the dirt road. Within minutes, the carcass flowed red with ants. But when Grandpa Phillips lay in the living room of Grandma's house, Royce was so worked up he grabbed the bars of the bedstead and rocked the bed so violently Aunt Paddy came in and slapped him on the thigh.

It was the last time my family dressed a body, scented it with after-shave, kept it with us while we talked and ate and listened to the radio broadcast out of Tyler. My mother made it the last time. But I do remember how it was, sitting in the rocker, listening to the shoes scuff across the wooden floor, men coming in from outside, knocking mud from their boots. My father came into the bedroom and led Royce and me into the kitchen. He gripped my arm with thick fingers and hurried Royce along in front of us. Dad seemed much stronger then, before the desk jobs, and toughened by the winter he spent in Korea more than a decade earlier. When I brushed against him on that day it seemed he had never quite shaken the scent of wet, woolen army blankets and Pall Mall cigarettes.

My mother sat on the edge of the tan couch, her hair stiff and full from a recent perm, and she seemed wary of leaning back against anything for fear her hair might break. She wore a short, dark dress that came up too high on her legs, revealing the satin band of her white slip. Her skin was flushed and thickened around her eyes from crying silent, difficult tears. I looked into the kitchen. Uncle Wayne was adding a leaf to the table. Aunt Paddy stood close to him with a stack of blue plates in her hands. I glanced at the dark casket, and though I could not see his face, I knew Great-Grandpa Phillips was lying there, like a white bulldog in a submarine.

It was early morning. We sat around the kitchen table. My father and Uncle Wayne drank black, chicory coffee and smoked Luckies. Aunt Paddy talked to my mother about allergies and how the pine pollen was carried north by the winds, all the way from East Texas to Kansas City and that we were somehow linked by this pollen, though she couldn't say how exactly. Grandma took off her rubber gloves and cooked big powdery biscuits in a Dutch oven. Royce tried to kick me under the table but found his legs weren't long enough after the leaf was added.

From where I sat, I could see the end of the casket. The handles were roughly cut. Places to get a good grip, and nothing more. I was not thinking about him rising up, looking at me through spectacles, moaning and pointing, floating around the ceiling, like ghosts of the dead did in movies, or hovering over the breakfast table while we sopped puddles of syrup from our plates. I wondered instead, only because he was in the very next room, if Grandpa Phillips was wearing his brown, Sunday-best dress shoes.

Then Uncle Jesse burst through the front door with his girlfriend riding on his back. At least I think of them coming in at that moment, me staring at the end of the casket. I cannot ever think of Uncle Jesse without seeing that brown box in the corner of my eye. Sometimes, I cannot distinguish, through the haze of years, if it belongs to him or Grandpa Phillips. Their deaths are mingled in my memory.

Jesse was the youngest of the three brothers, his face always red from the sun and wind, his body hardened by the work he did for the county highway department, spreading gravel and driving a road-grader. He held a Gibson guitar by the neck, out from his body and safely away from the kicking feet of the girl he carried. Uncle Jesse could play anything with strings. Grandma once said he could play "Little Brown Jug" on a pair of shoelaces. "Under the Double Eagle" was his specialty, though, and no matter how close I sat to him when he played, some strings seemed to sound without ever being touched.

Her name was Eudora. She had short, red hair held close to her head by a green bandanna. Her father was a missionary in South America and hadn't been seen since 1959. She told me once he had been eaten, but most certainly prayed over beforehand. She slid off Uncle Jesse's back and kissed my grandma on the temple. In a moment she was making her way around the table, kissing everyone on the cheek. My father leaned his head down to get his on the back of his neck. My mother held out her hand instead. She never liked Eudora and it wasn't until after Grandma died and Uncle Jesse was listed as missing in action in 1968 that she finally gave in and told her so.

I waited for Eudora and felt her warm lips on the side of my face, and a pleasant ache running to my lower back.

We ate thick maple syrup over our biscuits and talked about the cold air outside, about how much Great- Grandpa Phillips hated winter, and how Uncle Wayne was trying to get out of the hog business. Things had been good for a while, but Vietnam was not generating the demand for pork Korea had. "I don't know what they feed them," he said.

"Powdered substitutes," my father said. "That and corned beef hash. Some things don't change."

Grandma finally sat down to her own breakfast. Her upper lip wrinkled harshly as she sipped at the hot coffee. "Hogs or no hogs, that is the question." Aunt Paddy laughed out loud, sloshing coffee onto the table.

"It's time to make some decisions," Mother suddenly said. She took her empty plate from the table and dropped it into a tub of water by the sink.

It was quiet but for Grandma's smacking, then Uncle Wayne said he knew someone who owned a backhoe and would dig good grave for thirty dollars.

"That's steep," Uncle Jesse said.

Mother dropped another plate into the soapy water to let everyone know she didn't care what got broken.

I learned much later in my life that she went back home to Houston several times to get away from pine sap and gritty floors and tobacco. My father met her there when he was seventeen and she was sixteen. His father died of cancer in 1945, sitting straight-backed on the couch, two weeks after the war in Europe ended. That was why Dad was in Houston, working for the railroad, sweeping boxcars, sending half his check home. Shortly after they were married, he lost his job to a returning soldier who was missing part of his chin. But with the war over, with the housing boom that followed, a local saw mill agreed to hire him and they moved in with Grandma. Years later, long after we moved away for good, after my father's heart finally gave into cigarettes and Kentucky bourbon, Mother told me she begged him to stay in Houston and attend night school. "It wasn't that I didn't like your grandmother," she said. "I just wanted to move the family forward, but she held them," showing me both fists, "like posts driven into hard ground."

But it wasn't just Grandma. There were generations of woodcutters, bean farmers, cotton farmers, loggers, and preachers. There were the bounty hunters, those who killed off the red wolves for a pair of ears worth five dollars at the co-op. There were moonshiners and stock thieves. Some were musicians, banjo and mandolin players who learned music on the chipped, water-damaged keys of a Baptist church piano. It was their presence, though diffused and hidden, she fought against. They hung in our collective memory like spiderwebs, and she swept them out with a broom, only to find them rebuilding the next morning with my father expecting breakfast to be made for him, or Uncle Wayne bringing a raccoon home to smoke for dinner.

Mother disappeared after washing the dishes and went to Aunt Paddy's, leaving me to play Gin Rummy with my father, Uncle Wayne, Uncle Jesse, and Eudora. Royce stayed in the living room to keep Great-Grandpa Phillips company. Uncle Wayne slipped cards in and out of his socks, shifting his eyes, but no one said anything.

Late in the afternoon, two men arrived at Grandma's house. I recognized Brother Bean by his deep voice. He was the pastor of Saints Rest Baptist Church, a skinny man with a powerful, boney handshake. Eudora sat beside me on the couch and whispered into my ear that preachers could sense death miles from the body. I felt that ache in my lower back again and leaned closer to her, letting my elbow rest lightly against her thigh.

"This is Mr. Cassill," Mother said. "He has agreed to handle the ceremony."

"For a pretty penny," Eudora whispered, soft enough that only I heard her. Someone lit the stove in the kitchen to heat the house. I felt as if I were wearing a hot iron mask.

Mr. Cassill was a young man then, short and dark-skinned with a high forehead and eyes set low in his face. He wore a dark tweed suit and a thin red tie. I saw him many times after that day, to bury my grandmother, my father, Uncle Jesse. I even invited him to dinner after my father died. His delicate, wrinkled hands circled the plate in slow, deliberate movements, and I wasn't able to eat, thinking of those same hands carefully buttoning my father's wool trousers and gray herringbone jacket.

"Hello, Eugene," Uncle Wayne said. He sat with his arm around Aunt Paddy. "How's the wife?"

Mr. Cassill nodded and said: "Fine." He carried a thin sheen of perspiration over his upper lip.

Uncle Wayne nodded back at him as if to say he was pleased by the news. My father slid in the front door and went quietly into the kitchen, clutching the car keys in his hand, bent over with indigestion. Mother stood in the middle of the room with her arms crossed. Her permed and sprayed hair had softened a little since morning, though she still moved her head stiffly, as if wearing a heavy crown she feared might tumble off with any lapse in concentration.

Mr. Cassill examined the casket, ran his fingers along the seams, tested the handles, flattened his palms against the sides, moving first with, then against the grain. I wanted to tell him I had faith in the handles. "Of course, we can add some trim if you want, just to dull the edges before placing it in the viewing room," he said, in a soft, feminine voice.

Eudora fidgeted beside me on the couch. She smelled of Ivory soap.

Mother nodded to Mr. Cassill. "That would be nice," she said. "And I've asked Mrs. Beasley to be the organist."

"Jesse should play the guitar," Grandma said. She had grown sadder as the day wore on, with nothing left on Grandpa Phillips to dress up.

Eudora suddenly piped up and said she thought that was a grand idea, and that we could just as well have the ceremony right where we were, save on the funeral expenses, and walk to the cemetery for the burial. "All we need is a wagon to transport Mr. Phillips, and we could walk behind it. Like on TV when they buried President Kennedy.

"And," she said, "I'd take a good six-string guitar over a church organ any day," then she nudged me and asked didn't I think that was a good plan, and because she smiled at me and teasingly tugged at my earlobe, I nodded my head in agreement. "I'd like to see horse pull a wagon," I said.

Then my mother told me and Royce to go into the back bedroom and close the door while the grown-ups had a talk. I saw the flush blooming along her neck, the way it always did when she was upset.

I followed Royce into the bedroom, closed the door, but only enough to make it look closed. I sat on the floor and listened at the small opening.

"What are you up to?" Royce said, so I shushed him and told him to talk in a whisper. He said he didn't care a hoot about a funeral anyway, and he grabbed an old yarn doll off Grandma's dresser, lay down on the bed, and tossed the doll into the air and caught it over and over again.

While I couldn't make out much of what was said, I could tell it was Mother and Eudora doing all of the talking. No one else said a word, at least that I could hear. But I could see the front door, and after a few minutes I saw Eudora standing at it and about to leave. She had her hand on the knob, then let go and turned around. I heard her say, "We'll all be something different from now on," then something I couldn't make out, then she said, "There will be no real dying for any of us from now on. We'll hide from it all and fidget in our folding funeral home chairs and hope nothing ever hurts us and let hired hands do the important work for us." Then she turned, pushed open the door, and left it open behind her.

There was a long silence before Mother walked over to close the door, and then asked Mr. Cassill if he'd like some coffee. "Yes," he said. "It's been cold all day."

They took him early the next morning. I heard them grunting, straining to get the box through the narrow front door. "Tilt it sideways," one of them said. I think it was Uncle Jesse.

The thing I could identify, put my finger on, pinpoint with absolute accuracy, I saw only inside the blue-shingled house, in Grandma's bedroom, in the kitchen, in the room with the tan couch and the maple-colored casket, not when I wore my new suit from the Sears and Roebuck Boys Collection and sat in Cassill's Funeral Home. Royce sat beside me in a navy-blue suit my mother bought for him, though his pant legs were much too short. Aunt Paddy and Uncle

Wayne sat in the pew with my mother, grandmother, and father, all of them dressed in dark colors except for the pink nylon scarf Aunt Paddy tied around her neck. Uncle Jesse sat in a pew behind them, alone, but hoping Eudora would show up.

Organ music droned from behind a stiff curtain. I sat low in the pew and watched Mrs. Beasley's thick foot move across the black pedals, pressing out background chords for "Amazing Grace" and "Abide with Me." They kept the casket closed until the service began and I thought about what Eudora said, about funeral homes being a rip-off and considered the possibility Great-Grandpa Phillips might not be in the box. But with the lid open, I saw the tip of his nose, which had an unnatural, rosey hue.

When we passed by the casket, I thought how beautiful he looked, how tight and youthful his skin, down to the skin of his finger joints, normally rough from working without gloves, now beige and taut, like they were painted. He might have been a bookkeeper, or a store clerk, rather than a farmer.

Mother leaned over and removed his spectacles, tucking them into a tiny purse hanging from her wrist. Grandma passed by without looking down, staring instead at the pictures on the wall of Christ and the Resurrection, and Christ as a shepherd, surrounded by thick, flawless sheep.

Saints Rest Baptist Church was the family burial ground and only a quarter of a mile up the road from where my grandmother lived. Spanish moss hung from the limbs of the great pines. The cemetery was full of old Prussian immigrants from Oderberg and Dahlhausen, Tubbe's and Kolb's, with first names of Johann, Friedrich, Augustus. There was a corner reserved in the cemetery for us, the next generations, marked by a single pine tree, and extending past the tree to the chain-link fence.

Mr. Cassill delivered the body in a long black hearse. They slid the casket along a series of aluminum rollers. I think of two things now: T.V. dinners being loaded on a commercial airplane and Eudora waiting for Uncle Jesse's body to come rolling from a C-140.

The box came to rest above a green tarp that covered the hole. The mound of dirt beside the grave was draped with a green rug. I overheard Mr. Cassill telling Uncle Jesse that the roller system would revolutionize the funeral business like Ford's assembly line changed heavy industry. Mother wore a black veil and bought Grandma a big black hat to cover her grey hair. The hat had a long drawstring, tied too tightly, that bunched her face into deep wrinkles and made her look like an old man. Uncle Wayne, Uncle Jesse, and my father wore white corsages provided by the funeral home. Pastor Bean volunteered to be the fourth pall bearer, just to even things out, and he wore a corsage as well.

Eudora skipped the funeral service, but I saw her sitting cross-legged on the ground outside the cemetery gate, strummimg an occassional chord on Uncle Jesse's guitar. Pastor Bean quoted long passages from the Bible, and after he said a prayer, Mother scattered daisies over the casket, giving the last two to Royce and me to press in memory books.

When it was over, we walked back to my grandmother's house, with the exception of Uncle Wayne and my father, who stayed behind to help clean up. Grandma walked arm in arm with Aunt Paddy, telling her that she, Grandma, would be the next to go, but at least when the time came she wouldn't have to walk back home.

Before we reached the house where the Ladies Auxilliary had prepared a meal for the family, Eudora caught up and walked beside me. She took my hand in hers, and when I looked down I saw, despite the chilly air, she wasn't wearing shoes. She had turned her hair hankerchef into a headband, and she wore a sleeveless leather vest with long fringes. I gave her the daisy Mother had given me and she put it behind her ear.

The last time I saw Eudora was when Jesse's remains came off the airplane, but we didn't speak that day. She looked in my direction a couple of times and I made one feeble wave to catch her attention, but she looked right past me, and I heard later that she left the country shortly thereafter, although no one knew exactly where she went. Royce, who became a county deputy sheriff and patrolled those same dirt roads where we rode bikes when we visited my grandmother's house in later summers, claimed she went to Africa to find her father and ended up married to a Zulu chieftain. I thought that was just the kind of thing Royce would make up.

While Eudora and I walked side by side, Royce ran ahead and tried to get my attention by throwing rocks at my feet. They bounced off my shins and left white marks on my shiny black shoes. But all I thought about was the hand in my hand, and Great-Grandpa Phillips, surrounded by bright, yellow flowers, like the catbirds in the bar ditch.

We'll All Be Better People

By the time Frank's daughter texted him about the injured turkey, he had already had two substantial shots of Kentucky Bourbon and a tall can of his favorite Pilsner as a chaser. His phone pinged again, and the message read, *Call me?*, followed by a turkey emoji, followed by a wheelchair emoji.

He called.

"Are you coming?" Sam asked.

"What happened?"

"I hit a turkey on my way in. It's still alive."

"Like a Thanksgiving turkey?"

"A turkey turkey," she said. "A wild one. It's a tom."

"How do you know that?"

"I know a wild turkey when I see one."

Frank said, "No, I mean how do you know its name is Tom?"

"Cute," she said. "Are you coming or not? It's in the backseat of my car."

Frank imagined her car seats covered in feathers and blood and turkey shit. "Loose?" he asked.

"Of course not," she said. "He's in a seatbelt." He knew his daughter well enough to know that she might be telling the truth, or she might not be. Just like her mother, he thought. "He's wrapped in a blanket," she said. "I think he might be paralyzed."

"What do you expect me to do about it?" Frank said.

"I was thinking you could take him to that wildlife rescue place. I'd do it myself but I have to work. I can't lose the hours."

"Have you asked your mother?"

Sam said, "Her and Donny are in Mexico. They left two days ago."

"What the hell are they doing there?"

"What do you think they're doing? They went on a trip. Donny's company has a timeshare or something. I don't really know. So, are you coming or not? Hello?... Dad?"

Frank walked into the kitchen to get a few things together. It was a nearly four-hour drive to the animal rescue place in Lambert so he grabbed the Aldi's reusable grocery bag—something Nancy left behind when she moved out—and dropped in a package of saltines, a candy bar, a bottle of water, and the three cans of beer he had left in the fridge. The cans of beer were so cold he took one back out and drank it while he looked for his big travel cup. He didn't find it in the cabinet, so he took an old Sonic cup out of the kitchen trash, rinsed it, and filled it with ice. He slipped the bottle of bourbon into the bag as well, then walked to his truck parked in the driveway.

Prissy Walters, who lived next door, was outside watering her flowers. She didn't have any shoes on but wore a safari helmet and khaki shorts like the kind Frank remembered seeing in old movies about explorers going to Africa to shoot lions.

"Grocery day?" she asked. Then she bent the hose about six inches in to stop the flow.

"Yeah," Frank said. "There's a big meat sale going. I'm grilling steaks this weekend." Prissy and her husband, Gerald, used to come over for dinner on occasion, and since Prissy was a vegetarian and Gerald was a vegan, Nancy would go to lots of fuss to make sure everybody at the table ate only vegetarian and vegan for that dinner. Gerald ended up having a heart attack a year or so back, and went on full disability. Frank told Nancy he thought that was ironic, and she replied he shouldn't make fun of people who tried to improve themselves.

Prissy waved when he pulled out of the driveway. He waved back and saw her release the kink in the hose. The sudden burst of water stained her khaki shorts.

Sam worked at a pet store in a strip mall in Enid. She took care of the fish, lizards, and hamsters, stocked shelves, and sometimes worked the register. Frank knew she could do better, but she dropped out of college after her first semester. After that, she lived in a camper with a roughneck named Burl Wilson. When he went to Alaska to work the oil fields for three months, and then came home with another girlfriend, Sam moved back in with Frank and Nancy long enough to save for an apartment.

By that time Nancy had already decided she didn't want to be married anymore, so within a month of Sam's move, Nancy packed up and found an apartment as well, a nice one in the nicer part of town. She met Donny at a summer pool party for the residents. At least that's what he'd heard. Now, apparently, they were in Mexico somewhere.

Frank called her once, after Sam told him about Donny. It was a Sunday night. He wanted to tell her he was taking early retirement from the U.S. Postal Service, where he had worked the counter for the last eighteen years. "There won't be much money," he said. "I may have to sell the house."

Nancy coughed. Some people just cleared their throats to let you know they were about to say something they thought was important, but Nancy always let out a short, one note cough. He had pointed it out to her, but she didn't think it was such an odd tic. "I told you the house is yours," she said. "That means you get the house, and whatever goes with it. Lock, stock, and barrel."

"What the hell does that mean?" Frank said.

"Have you been drinking?" Nancy asked.

"What do you think?" Frank said, then, "Is that Donny a drinker?"

After a long silence, Nancy coughed and said, "We've cut ties, Frank. We can both aim to be better people now, can't we? Can we try to do that? For Sam's sake, at least?"

Frank felt his throat tightened. "Sam is goddamn near thirty years old, Nance. If she was nine, we could do it for her sake."

Frank pulled into the parking lot. Sam leaned against her car with her arms crossed. He turned into a space and rolled down his window. She was wearing her work uniform, navy blue scrubs with dog and cat silhouettes on the shirt pocket. Her face was splotchy along her jawline. It happened to her when she was stressed. "What took you so long?" she said.

"I was practicing my gobble in front of the mirror," he said, then, "I got here as soon as I could. Where's the bird?"

"Hold on," she said. She opened her car door and pulled out a large pet crate covered in a Winnie-the-Pooh blanket. She walked around and opened his passenger-side door.

"No, in the bed," he said, thumbing over his shoulder.

"Move your shit," she said. "He's riding up front with you."

Frank pulled the Aldi's bag to the space between the seats, and Sam slid the crate inside. She grabbed the shoulder belt, stretched it as far as it would go, pushed the crate hard against the seat back, and reached over to find the buckle. "I thought you were kidding about the seatbelt."

"I was," she said, pushing her hair off her forehead. "But it might make him calmer if the crate doesn't move around on the way there."

Frank looked at the crate. He couldn't see inside because of the blanket, and he heard no sound coming from it. "You sure he's still alive in there?"

"He's alive," she said. "I checked before you got here. He just doesn't move around much. That's pretty much the definition of 'paralyzed'. And I borrowed the crate from the storeroom, so make sure you bring it back, OK? It's fifty dollars, even with my discount, so *please* don't leave it down there. OK, Dad?"

"Anything else I can do to make him comfortable? Maybe I'll turn on the radio. What kind of music does he like?" Sam stared at him, expressionless, but then he saw she was tearing up a little. "I'll drive fast," he said.

She nodded, and swiped one eye with her sleeve. Her red splotches had travelled into her cheeks. "What's in the bag?"

"Travel supplies. In case me and Tom here get hungry." He thought she was going to ask to look in the bag, but she didn't.

"Call me when you get there?" she said finally, then gently closed the truck door.

CritterCare was located outside the town of Lambert. Sam had called ahead to make sure it was OK if he brought the turkey down. He keyed in the address on his phone, and he would arrive by 2:45, without any long stops or traffic hold-ups.

He reached into the Aldi's bag and took out a beer. It was still cold and he drank it and ate a few saltines. By the time he reached the interstate, he had eaten most of the saltines and drank the last beer. He was feeling happy about the drive. At first he thought it would be miserable, and he thought how silly it was to travel four hours to deliver what would likely be a dead turkey to an animal rescue. They'd see the Winnie-the-Pooh blanket and then the pet crate, and the limp body of the bird and wonder what the hell he was thinking coming all that way. Then they'd probably ask for a donation to help save the next turkey who did make it because that next person cared a little bit more and drove a little faster.

But he was retired now and had the time. Plus, Sam asked him to do it, and he figured he owed her a few good days for all the shitty ones he and Nancy had dropped on her.

On her recent birthday he took her to an Italian restaurant and ordered her favorite, linguini with alfredo sauce, and he had something with eggplant, and then he ordered two glasses of wine to have with the meal. She talked about work and her lousy store manager, and he took the opportunity to tell her he thought she might want to try college again, or maybe a trade school, and that he would cover her tuition. She could even live with him in the house again, take her old bedroom back.

Sam didn't take his suggestions in the spirit in which he intended them. She moved the soggy linguini around in the puddle of oily white sauce and barely ate any of it. "I do like my job," she said. "You think I shouldn't, but I do."

"Did your mother say I said that? That I said you shouldn't like your job? Well, I'm just fine with you liking your job. Tell her I'm fine with it, will you? Will you convey those sentiments for me?" Frank drained his wine glass and asked the waiter to bring a full bottle of the same.

Sam said, "You can just have mine."

"I don't want your birthday wine. It's yours to drink or not, just like your job."

"I think that's a really bad comparison," she said.

"I wasn't trying for a good one," Frank said. "I was just trying to tell you that you should keep your job at the pet store, and maybe drink off a little wine out of that glass. It's your birthday after all and I want you to be happy on your birthday. I want both of us to be happy about your birthday."

The waiter brought the bottle and Sam asked for the check, even though she wasn't paying. They left the restaurant. Frank took the bottle of wine and shoved it under the seat of his truck, then drove Sam back to her apartment.

At home he put the wine in the fridge. He figured he'd keep it there and then bring it out some day and tell her it was the special birthday bottle he saved from the Italian restaurant.

He tried calling her but it just went to voicemail. He waited another fifteen minutes and tried again, but she still didn't answer. He took the bottle of wine out of the fridge and started looking for the corkscrew. He wasn't much of a wine drinker, and when he did buy wine he always bought the kind with a screw-off cap. He looked in the utensil drawer, then the cabinets by the stove, but there was no corkscrew. Nancy must have taken it, he thought. He put the bottle back in the fridge.

He pulled the bourbon from the Aldi's bag, poured a couple of shots worth into the Sonic cup, sipped bourbon through the straw as he drove, and took a few bites of the candy bar.

He was at about the halfway mark so he left the interstate and stopped at a convenience store to use the restroom and pick up a few more snacks. He was a little buzzed from the beer and bourbon, but he had eaten all of the saltines and drank the bottle of water, so he felt pretty clear-headed. When he pulled into a space in front of the store, he saw a man sitting next to the trashcan. He had on a red ball cap stained with motor oil, and his pants were dirty and had big rips in the knees. He wore running shoes with thick soles but no socks. His ankles were thin and white. He held an empty Yoo-hoo bottle in one hand and an orange dog leash in the other. There was no dog attached.

Frank stepped out of the truck and the man said, "Warm today, Brother."

"Not bad," Frank said.

"If I had a dollar, I'd get me another cold drink."

"Might be a good idea at that," Frank said, then walked inside the store.

Frank went to the restroom, then searched the aisles. He picked up a package of salted peanuts, a bag of kettle chips, and then two bottles of water from a cooler filled with ice. He grabbed an egg salad sandwich, along with a two-pack of string cheese. The line at the register was pretty long so he was inside a good fifteen minutes.

He left the store, opened the driver's door of his truck, and tossed the sack of items inside the Aldi's bag. That's when he saw the pet carrier was gone. The Winnie-the-Pooh blanket was on the floorboard and part of the shoulder belt was wedged in the passenger door.

Frank took a quick look around parking lot, then walked the line of cars parked at the front of the store and looked through side windows and windshields. Then he walked around to the side of the store where a guy in a pink muscle shirt was airing up a tire.

"Excuse me, sir. Did you happened to see anyone with a pet carrier?"

The guy straightened up, opened his mouth, but just then the compressor kicked on, so Frank couldn't make out what he said at first. "Across the field," the man said again, and pointed to a broad expanse of wheat stubble that spread between the convenience store and what looked like an old auto repair shop.

Frank saw someone walking away. He saw the red cap, and the carrier in the guy's right hand.

Frank hadn't taken a quick step in years, but did his best to move from a walk to a slow jog. He felt the beer and bourbon and water slosh in his stomach, and he thought he might puke before he caught up. Finally, when he got close enough, he stopped, took as deep a breath as he could and yelled, "Hey, hey! You there! Hey, you!"

The man stopped and turned around. He raised his hand and waved. He didn't keep walking, but stood there until Frank caught up.

"How's it, Brother?" the man said.

Frank said, "You stole that from my truck, Buddy. That's my carrier, and that's my turkey in it. Hand it over or I'll call the cops."

The man lifted the carrier high enough to look through the wire door. Frank watched him stick his fingers through the wire. "What's wrong with it?" the man asked. Frank noticed he had tied the orange dog leash around his waist. "Did you shoot it or something?"

"Ran over it," Frank said. "Now hand it over."

The man looked at Frank, then back at the turkey. "I'd like to keep him," the man said. "I'd take good care of it."

"Well, you can't."

Then the man set the carrier on the ground, removed his hat, and raised his fists. "The way I see it, he's safer with me than you, Brother.'

The man took a step back and threw a couple of air punches in Frank's general direction, then turned around and did the same in the direction of the shop at the edge of the field.

The last thing Frank wanted to do was get in a fight with a guy older than was, and likely homeless, so he said, "Maybe we can come to an agreement? You carry the crate back to my truck and we'll cut a deal. I'll trade you for it."

The man slowly dropped his fists. "I'd expect more than the dollar I already asked you for and didn't get," he said, then he picked up the carrier and started walking.

Frank took the Aldi's bag out of his truck. He offered the man the peanuts and a bottle of water. The man said, "What else?" He offered the string cheese. The man said nothing. Finally, Frank held out the entire Aldi's bag. The man set the carrier on the ground, took the bag by one handle, and dug around inside. One item at a time, he held up the egg salad sandwich, the string cheese, the peanuts, the water, the chips, then the pint of bourbon.

He looked at the label on the bourbon bottle, then shook the bottle. He held it for a long time, but then put it back. He took the sandwich, both bottles of water, then handed Frank the bag. "Deal," the man said.

When he arrived at CritterCare he thought GPS had made a mistake. He pictured a stone or brick building, or at least something that looked like a clinic, or maybe something you might see at a zoo. There were a few chain-link pens, like at the dog pound, but the building was just an old house, its paint peeling in flakes along the wall slats, and an elevated porch with support posts that looked warped. It was a wonder, Frank thought, that the whole thing hadn't fallen in on itself.

He got out of his truck, steadied a little against the door, then walked around to the passenger side. He picked up the Winnie-the-Pooh blanket from the floorboard and covered the crate, then lifted it off the seat. He felt the turkey shift inside,

He walked up the steps and read a sign tacked on the door.

Please knock.
DO NOT ENTER WITH AN ANIMAL.

Frank set the crate on a long wooden bench and knocked, then sat down. After about a minute, he stood up and knocked again. The door opened. A young man with a thin beard and acne on his forehead stepped out. He wore glasses and a T-Shirt with a coyote on the front and a pair of loose-fitting cargo pants. "Can I help you?"

Frank stood up and pointed to the covered crate. "I brought a turkey," he said. "A wild turkey. My daughter called this morning? She hit it with her car."

"Hmmm," the man said.

"Not on purpose," Frank added.

The man nodded. Then he handed Frank a clip board and an ink pen. "Fill this out, OK? I'll take the bird and come back to talk." He lifted the blanket, peered inside, then flipped the blanket onto the bench. He took the crate inside and closed the door.

The form read **In-take** in bold, followed by questions about the animal, county of origin, condition of the animal, then name, address, phone numbers, home and work, of the person submitting the form, followed by a request for a donation.

On the blank line after "Condition," he wrote *Injured*, and he wrote Sam's phone number. For a second, he considered listing Nancy's number, but didn't. He wasn't even sure she had the same number anyway. He left the donation line blank.

It was uncomfortably warm on the porch. His head was beginning to ache. He was tired from the drive, and he wished he hadn't given away his water. He left the clipboard on the bench and walked down the steps to his truck. The Sonic cup had a little ice left, so he shook in into his mouth and held it until it melted. It tasted of weak bourbon. Then he vomited.

He sat on the ground and leaned against the front tire. He thought he may have passed out for a few seconds while sitting there, but he

86

wasn't sure. But the man with the glasses was standing over him and asking if he was OK. He held the clipboard, and a yellow folder.

"Just got too hot," Frank said. "I'm fine." Then he stood up. "How's the turkey?"

The man wiped his acned forehead and pushed his glasses higher on his nose. He was sweating and the coyote on his shirt was spotted like a Dalmatian. "The doctor is looking at him now, but I'd guess a spinal injury of some sort. Unfortunately," he said, taking off his glasses, "wild turkey don't do well in captivity. Even if he survives in the short term, his chances are pretty low." The man reminded Frank of an actor in a movie playing a surgeon who had to give the family bad news. Then he handed Frank a yellow folder and the carrier. "I cleaned it out with disinfectant." Before Frank closed the door, the man said, "We appreciate your kindness. Most people would have just let that bird die, you know?"

Frank nodded, and could only say, "Thank you," then started the engine.

He felt bad about leaving the donation line blank, and almost called the man back to hand him the little cash he had in his wallet, but he had already gone inside. He opened up the yellow folder and there was a brochure with pictures of baby squirrels and baby rabbits. Behind the brochure was a sheet of paper that looked like old-fashioned parchment. It was a certificate that read *CritterCare Hero*, and had a golden sunburst sticker, and was signed by a Dr. Beth Murphy, DVM.

Back on the highway, he thought about Nancy being in Mexico with Donny. He had never seen Donny. No one had ever even described him. He tried to imagine what someone named Donny might look like, but no one came to mind except Donny Osmond.

He thought he might try to call her. He had a few questions, like why she went to Mexico when she hated hot weather and didn't even like Mexican food. Also, he wanted to ask her what, exactly, had happened between them. He knew the obvious reasons, but he had been thinking lately that there might be other reasons she never mentioned. He'd like to know. Donny probably knew what those other reasons were by now. She was probably sitting in a restaurant in Mexico, eating food she didn't like and telling Donny all the reasons she had to leave her husband, Frank, after 35 years.

He thought about it for more than an hour, but decided not to call her.

He stopped at the convenience store again. He pulled up to the gas pump. The old guy with the red hat wasn't sitting out front. Frank filled up, then walked around the corner where the air hose was and saw him. He was sitting on the concrete, his legs straight out, his back against the wall, his hat covering his face. Frank heard him snore.

He walked to his truck, where he rolled up the Winnie-the-Pooh blanket and shoved it to the back of the pet carrier. Then he picked up the Aldi's bag and what was in it and pushed it inside as well. He closed the wire door and toted the carrier to the side of the store. He left it next to the sleeping man.

Back in the truck he called Sam.

"Where have you been?" she asked. She sounded groggy, like she just woke up "How'd it go? What did they say about the turkey? Did he live? Will he?"

"There's always a possibility," Frank said. He came to the on ramp to the interstate and the truck headlights switched on and the dashboard lit up. By the time he got home it would be completely dark, he thought, except where he sat, hands resting on the wheel, the cab holding all the light in. "It's possible," he said again, thinking maybe she hadn't heard him. "I wouldn't bet against it."

If Nothing Happens Like It Should

When I was fourteen I thought I plugged one with a 20-gauge slug. She was only ten feet away. I was dreaming and building little houses and forts and corrals out of sticks. The big rock I sat on was covered with moss, like green indoor/outdoor carpet, and I tore little squares off and made green roofs. I was always messing around.

We saw each other at the same time, and she looked at me the same way I looked at her, only she looked for a good thirty seconds and then forgot what she was looking at. Deer will do that.

There was another with her. I heard it walking on the other side of a Blackjack tangle. But you can't turn a head or blink an eye or swallow or breathe too hard through your nose, otherwise it will know something is up and just leave you shaking like you were having a seizure.

I thought the dumbest thing: maybe it was another hunter who just looked like a deer. That was how much of a haze I was looking through, that dreamy feeling you get when you go to bed too late and get up too early and your eyes ache from being open too long. She just appeared, and very close to me, even though I was playing around and moving my arms and head just like you aren't supposed to do.

Brother Ed was sitting in a tree about fifty yards away. I saw his orange hat about halfway up. It was a stupid hat, with long ear flaps and a strap that went under his chin, only his chin was too thick, and the strap just hung down beside his cheek. He had his back to me. Brother Ed hunted with us all the time, with Daddy and me, since his son wouldn't pull a trigger. That just about tore him up. Even now, Ronnie calls me up and asks how his dad is doing. I tell him fine, although I'd like to tell him Ed just can't get over him not being able to squeeze a trigger. But I always just let it pass, say goodbye, and hang up. That's Ed's problem.

I could pull a trigger, so Brother Ed couldn't face up to that because of Ronnie. I proved I could jerk a trigger the year before when a spike buck trotted into the middle of a winter wheat patch and I laid a bead on him. But instead of going for a safe lung shot I tried for a dead-on heart shot and ended up hitting the dirt right under his belly. I didn't have another slug in the gun or I would have had plenty of time for another try; that buck just stood there shaking, like he was having a fit of nerves. That was the first season after Daddy bought my shotgun for $36. The salesman sold it cheap since it was the floor model and was scratched on the stock and butt. It was only a single shot, and I didn't think I'd get my hands into my vest for another shell without falling out of the tree. The thing that got me was the thought of him running away just about the time I did manage to get another shell in. So I didn't even try. If I had tried, I probably would have pegged him. I think Daddy finally scared him away when he climbed out of his tree a hundred yards or so to the east to see if I got one. The proper thing to do was for him to stay put in the tree for at least thirty minutes. That way if I made a good shot, which I didn't on that occasion, the buck would eventually lay down and bleed out. If you jump them when they are just about bled out but have enough life in them to run a good hundred yards or so, you end up with no trail to follow and the coyotes find them before you do.

The doe was closer than that buck, though. Almost closer to me than I was to myself. Any closer and she would have been on the other side. That close. I raised the gun to my cheek, even though the thought she might really just be a stray dog or coyote or nothing at all was still in my mind. You can't ever be sure for some reason, no matter what you believe you see. Sometimes cows are colored like deer. Sometimes squirrel hunters aren't smart enough to wear orange and they traipse around in brown vests and brown hats and brown pants. And because your brain is so scattered from excitement you never really know anything for sure. All I know was I didn't even have to aim, she was so close. I just leveled the barrel at her shoulder and pulled back the hammer. I know she heard the click because her ears flicked a little, like they would when nothing worse than a fly was about to land on her. Then, all the sudden, it was like every leaf of every limb on every tree shook. Of course, it was me getting knocked around. Those slugs shoot hard.

My ears buzzed for a good full minute. A real high-pitched tone over a real low-pitched tone, with a cushion of air in-between. That was what I heard. I didn't hear my heart beat but I felt it, even through all the layers of clothes: the long johns, the flannel shirt, the coat, the blaze orange vest. I felt the beats on the outside. It was beating that hard.

I sat where I was for a minute. For some reason I thought she's fall right where she was. But she was gone just like she showed up, right out of the air, and then right back into it.

Brother Ed started out of his tree. I saw his orange hat moving down a little at a time. He sent some limbs down, too, and that made him so nervous it took a good ten minutes for him to climb the eight or nine feet to the ground. Ed was too big to be in trees anyway. The year before he skinned the hell out of his hands when a limb broke under him and he did a fireman's slide down the trunk. It was a cold day, too, and Ed didn't make a sound his hands hurt so bad, because he knew how terrible a sound he would make.

He walked up to my rock and looked down at the little stick houses with green moss for roofs. Then he pushed his orange cap back on his head. "Did a buck come out?" he asked. I told him no. I only saw the doe, but I heard another one behind me. He fiddled with his cap again, taking it off to smooth back his black hair. He wore hair oil and Aqua Velva even when he went hunting. He just stood there until he saw Daddy coming across a little divide. Daddy was looking along the ground as he walked, like he picked up a blood trail. Before he even got to us, Brother Ed leaned toward me and said, "If you went to church Wednesday nights you might have better luck," then he propped against a tree and waited. I thought Brother Ed was mad because I got a shot not fifty yards from him, and that I was goofing off and breaking twigs and moving around. I did everything you aren't supposed to do to be a successful deer hunter. Brother Ed thought deer hunting was both a science and something that works out by the grace of God. I didn't fall under either category. I thought I had him figured out, but when Daddy got to us Brother Ed said: "He shot a doe," without looking over his shoulder at me, or using my name.

Daddy looked at Ed, and then at me still sitting on the rock, and then back at Ed. "Maybe a button buck, he said. "Did you see buttons?"

I came right out and told him it was a doe. When I told him how close she was I thought he'd understand. They just don't come that close and still give you a chance. The whole thing was a freak. Nothing was like it should be, I said. The fact that it was a does fit right in with the whole weird thing. It was like she was being offered to me. I could have touched her with the barrel. She was that close.

Brother Ed said it was not a button buck, like I hadn't already made that clear enough, and that he saw two does to his right and he was hoping a buck would follow them out of the brush. Bucks do that. They let the does walk into the open first, and if nothing happens they come out, too. I thought Brother Ed was just being spiteful because his boy couldn't pull a trigger to save his own life.

I told Daddy she came up the hill, and there was another behind me but I didn't turn around knowing what would happen if I did. He didn't smile or tell me it was the thing to do, but turned around and said we needed to look for some blood and that maybe I missed. I told him I hit her square somewhere, but I didn't see her run off in any particular direction because of the shotgun's kick, but he was already walking around with his eyes on the fallen leaves looking for something to track. "Most likely gut shot," he said. Did she hunch over?" I said I didn't see her, but thought I made a good lung shot. He said, "If we find blood with bubbles, then we'll call it a lung shot. But if we find dark blood . . ." He didn't finish what he was saying but pulled out his red bandana to blow his nose. At least he was looking.

If there was snow on the ground we probably would have picked up her trail right away, but the ground was covered in bone-dry oak leaves. You always see people tracking deer in the snow, but where I come from it never snows early as rifle season, so you have to be a better tracker than usual. Daddy told Brother Ed to look for shine and not color, but Brother Ed was meandering around like he dropped something out of his pocket that he didn't care if he found or left to rot in the woods. That was how hard he tried to find a blood trail.

After a good twenty minutes Brother Ed walked up behind me and Daddy and said it would be better if we didn't find her since the game ranger always patrolled the area so much during rifle season, and none of the three of us had a doe tag.

Daddy acted like he didn't hear him, but I could tell he thought Ed might be right. But then he said, "I think he missed anyway." I started to say Brother Ed wasn't covering the ground very good, but I didn't. I said I thought we should make a bigger loop since she might not drop any blood for a good fifty yards or more. They both looked at me. Daddy looked like he felt sorry for me but was mad at me at the same time for taking aim at a doe, and Brother Ed looked at me like I was a nuisance and didn't understand anything about the natural ways of whitetail deer, or how a shot deer acted. After a minute, Daddy said she might have walked over the ridge and laid down to die. He talked Ed into going to the right for a hundred yards and then doubling back while he went to the left and circled. I was told to walk straight through the middle until I got to the bottom of the shallow ravine where we would all meet up. Brother Ed pulled his hat down over his eyes and left without saying a word. I knew he wasn't going to try very hard because I saw him looking up in the trees instead of on the ground when he walked away. If I had plugged a squirrel he might have found something.

I put my gloves on and loaded another shell into the chamber of the shotgun. Before we left home that morning I picked out three shells to call lucky. The luckiest I already used, since they say the first shot is the one that counts most. The second didn't have to be so lucky, and the third didn't matter much at all. But I had them marked one, two, three, just to keep things orderly like it was supposed to be. I cradled the gun in such a way so I could bring it up and get off a quick shot if I needed one. I even opened the chamber twice just to make sure I had reloaded because my mind was not really clear by then with all that was going on.

The wind was blowing hard into my face. It was cold, but under all my clothes I was sweating from being nervous and walking so much. I knew the ravine ended in a dry stream bed about a hundred and fifty yards downhill. I thought maybe she ran the length of the ravine instead of trying to climb out the other side. If that was the case we were all going in the wrong direction. I decided to walk to the bottom, cross the stream bed, and then go parallel on the other side. That way I might pick up her trail no matter which direction she took.

I did some stalking, covering only a hundred yards or so in a long hour. Take two steps and stop. Wait. Listen. Wait some more. Take two steps and stop. All the time I kept my eyes on the ground. The thing about tracking is you spend all your time looking down, and you might as well have blinders on when it comes to direction. I looked around after I stalked and tracked a while, and couldn't figure out exactly where I was. The funny thing is, even if you turn around and look for a tree you just passed you never can figure out which one it was, since now you're looking at it from the other side, and trees have entirely different personalities from one side to the next.

You wouldn't think somebody could get very lost in a hundred yards. You always think a football field being a hundred yards long and nobody ever gets lost walking on a football field. But a hundred yards of Blackjack oak and briar is a different story. So there I was, not wanting to yell out because they'd know I was turned around. But I think I was more afraid nobody would answer and I'd know I was lost for sure. I thought about the direction of the sun, but since I didn't know where the sun was before I got lost it didn't do any good where it was after I was lost. I stood in one spot for twenty minutes or so, afraid to move one way or the other, afraid Brother Ed was watching me and laughing, the way some deacons do, or if I moved one step in either direction, that one step might take me out of somebody's line of sight. I figured I walked more than a hundred yards because I was already nervous. I probably walked two hundred since I crossed the dry stream bed a half hour back. I did a one-eighty and found the stream bed again, only there it was wet and puddled in places. I was way off line and might wander all day thinking I was heading for the road when I was really running at an angle and might not find the road at all.

So I stood against a tree, wondering how long it would be before they started to worry about me. It was still only about two o'clock, but before long the sky would turn orange and I'd have to think about it getting dark, and I was already tired from no sleep the night before and no lunch.

And then I saw her, like she came out of the air again. Her head was almost dragging the ground. Her legs were shaking under her and her whole body was quivering and jerking around. It was like she needed to throw up or something, or drop a fawn. I thought I saw a dark patch of blood just behind her shoulder, but my mind was scattered again and she might have just been half covered in shadow, and that made her look splotched. She was not breathing so much as snorting, making the leaves and dirt move with her nose so close to the ground. There was even some old leaves stuck to her nose. I thought maybe she was going to fall down, but before I even got it clear in my head that I needed to finish her off, she raised her head straight up and turned to look at me. It was not like before when she looked at me then forgot about me. She didn't move her head at all, and her body didn't shake anymore and I couldn't hear her breathing anymore. She was perfectly still, like hunters are supposed to be when they wait for deer. That was the way she was being still, like I'd forget her and just go about my business. Right then I knew the whole thing wasn't right because I did exactly what you aren't supposed to do: I took my eyes off her and looked down at me feet, at my boot laces, at the round little eye-holes where the laces passed through, and at the double knot I always tied to keep the laces from flopping around. I had the strangest feeling in my legs and I couldn't make my feet fit into those boots.

When I finally looked up again it was almost dark, and I was sitting on the ground with my legs crossed under me and dead to the world of touch. The skin on my face was numb from the wind, and I must have banged against my knees when I fell because my nose bled and the blood dried out around my mouth. The breech was open on my shotgun, and my second lucky shell was missing and there was just a wad of grass in the chamber.

I yelled as loud as I could. Just bawled out like Ed would sound if he let loose after sliding bare-handed down a tree trunk on a freezing cold day. I let out like Ronnie might have let out if he pulled a trigger against any living thing on the planet. Every leaf on every limb on every tree seemed to shake I yelled so loud, and I don't think I let go the last good one until I was sitting on the hood of Brother Ed's blue station wagon with Daddy trying to feed me an aspirin.

Brother Ed told me in the car on the way home I must have missed the doe. But sometimes deer come back to see who shot at them, he said. They are such curious creatures, he said. I told him I messed around too much and couldn't be still or quiet to save my life, and that I always turned my head this time and that every time a leaf rattled. I needed to learn how to shift my eyes from one side to the next without moving my whole head. On top of that I needed to practice with the shotgun, or maybe save up for a rifle like his, with a good scope, since I missed two deer in two seasons. I said a person can't be successful if nothing happens like it should. He said he was happy I thought so.

About the Author

Paul Bowers is the author of a previous collection of short fiction, *Like Men, Made Various* (Lost Horse Press), and three poetry collections. He lives with his family on a small farm in northwest Oklahoma.

Also by Paul Bowers

Fiction
Like Men, Made Various

Poetry
The Lone, Cautious, Animal Life
Occasional Hymns
Ten Acres of the Universe